Amelia woke screaming...

She detected the same acrid odor she'd smelled that night. Smoke and fire!

In her cabin.

She jumped up, grabbing at clothes, her camera bag and her tote. Then she heard a shout outside her door.

"Amelia, wake up!"

Marco Landon, the private investigator. Marco was here, and the cabin was on fire. A shooter earlier and now this. Someone was after her.

She tried to call out, but still weak from the dream, she couldn't find her voice or her breath. She didn't want to pass out. She had to get out of here.

"Amelia?"

The locked door to her room crashed open and Marco came toward her, grabbed her tote and camera bag out of her hands, then lifted her up and into his arms, shielding her face as he ran back through the breezeway and hurried toward the only exit not on fire. But the door to the back deck was jammed. Marco couldn't get it to budge...

With over seventy books published and millions in print, **Lenora Worth** writes award-winning romance and romantic suspense. Three of her books finaled in the ACFW Carol Awards, and her Love Inspired Suspense novel *Body of Evidence* became a *New York Times* bestseller. Her novella in *Mistletoe Kisses* made her a *USA TODAY* bestselling author. Lenora goes on adventures with her retired husband, Don, and enjoys reading, baking and shopping...especially shoe shopping.

Books by Lenora Worth

Love Inspired Suspense

Undercover Memories
Amish Christmas Hideaway
Amish Country Secret
Retribution at the Ranch

Rocky Mountain K-9 Unit

Christmas K-9 Unit Heroes
"Hidden Christmas Danger"

True Blue K-9 Unit: Brooklyn

Deadly Connection

True Blue K-9 Unit

Deep Undercover

Visit the Author Profile page at LoveInspired.com for more titles.

RETRIBUTION AT THE RANCH

LENORA WORTH

LOVE INSPIRED SUSPENSE

INSPIRATIONAL ROMANCE

LOVE INSPIRED® SUSPENSE
INSPIRATIONAL ROMANCE

ISBN-13: 978-1-335-58746-6

Recycling programs
for this product may
not exist in your area.

Retribution at the Ranch

For questions and comments about the quality of this book, please contact us at CustomerService@Harlequin.com.

Love Inspired
22 Adelaide St. West, 41st Floor
Toronto, Ontario M5H 4E3, Canada
www.LoveInspired.com

Printed in U.S.A.

He that believeth on me, as the scripture hath said,
out of his belly shall flow rivers of living water.
—*John* 7:38

To my Texas friends and fellow writers—
Eve Gaddy and Janet Justiss.
Thank you for your love and support, always!

ONE

"**W**ho are you and what are you doing here?"

Amelia Garcia had moved to Caddo Lake in East Texas to get away from the world. Now someone was messing with her. After spotting the hulking figure moving outside the window, she'd grabbed her Remington and carefully made her way through the glass-walled breezeway between the bedroom and the main part of the cabin. A rifle came in handy in these isolated woods where cypress trees cast dark shadows on the water and wild animals roamed day and night, looking for prey.

But this intruder was human.

He held up his hands, one holding a gun. "Hey, are you Amelia Garcia?" he asked as if he was delivering a package.

Noting he wasn't going for a shootout, she asked, "Who are you?"

"You first," he said. "I'm looking for Amelia Garcia?"

"Why?"

He let out a huff of aggravation. "I'm Marco Landon, a private investigator from Austin. I was hired to locate Amelia Garcia. And if you *are* her, then you're one hard woman to find."

Amelia stepped closer and aimed the gun at his chest. "Maybe I don't want to be found."

He gave her a tired stare, then held his gun away from her. "If you'll put down the gun, I'll show you my credentials."

"First, why are you carrying a gun?"

"Uh, well, we're in Texas, I have a permit, and I wasn't sure I had the right address." He shrugged. "And…gators, snakes, things like that tend to make me a little anxious." He shook his head. "And then, there's a woman who knows how to use a rifle now holding that rifle on me."

She came closer, the rifle leading the way. "Cut the cute and tell me what you want."

He let out a long-suffering sigh. "I'm here on behalf of the lawyer for Leo Colón."

That stopped Amelia cold. "Which lawyer?"

"Samuel Chastain."

She remembered Sam. He'd been Leo's sidekick. "Why does he need to talk to me?" she asked, her heart skipping a few beats. No one was supposed to know where she was.

The man came closer, giving her a chance to take a good long look at him in the muted porch light. Dark shaggy hair and deep, dark eyes. About six inches taller than her five foot five, dressed in an aged leather jacket and black shirt. A tall drink of water—that's what any red-blooded woman would call him. He looked haggard, weary and earnest.

But could she trust him?

He grunted. "Look, I'm tired and it's kind of chilly

out here." He held his gun down. "I'll be happy to explain everything and let you check out my credentials."

She nodded. "What does Chastain want with me?"

The man—Marco—glanced up at her. "I'm sorry to say your uncle passed away two weeks ago. We've been trying to find you since."

Amelia gasped and went weak, but she held the rifle tight, her left hand white knuckling the barrel, her right index finger shaking against the trigger. "What are you telling me?"

Marco opened his mouth to answer when shots rang out and the porch column next to Amelia's head splintered from a bullet hit. Then the second one whizzed past her and knocked out a windowpane. Before she could react, he dived at her and took her down onto the porch. "Get inside. Now!"

Marco crouched and dragged her and her rifle inside the house, but she yanked herself away and fired the rifle like a determined soldier crawling back onto a battlefield.

He shut the door before she could run out, then slid down to block it with his body. "Stop."

"Someone is shooting at you," she replied from her spot in the hallway, her green eyes wide, her nostrils flaring with anger. "I want them to understand they can't do that on my property."

"Me? I think they might be shooting at you. Maybe someone else is looking for you, too."

She shifted to sit next to him against the door, her breath rising, and stared at him as if she still considered shooting him. "Nobody has bothered me here for the last three years and now, it's getting crowded out there."

Marco slid his handgun into his shoulder holster. "Look, I'm one of the good guys. I've been looking for you all over Texas, know what I mean? A lot of territory to cover. I'm tired, I need to sleep about a week and I'm starving for a steak—medium rare—and some scrambled eggs with habanero sauce. And a big cup of strong coffee."

The woman—Amelia—gave him a good long stare, her eyes moving over him like a cat about to pounce, waves of burnished brown hair falling around her face. "Tell me what happened to Leo."

He helped her up, then checked the nearest window. "I will, but first we have to make sure our company's left." Looking over his shoulder, he added, "You might want to report this."

"No."

"Why not?"

"I hope my shots scared them away," she said, her hand moving over her hair to rearrange it. "And I really don't want the attention. You know, sirens and sheriff deputies walking around. I like to keep a low profile." She paused and then said, "What I would like is the truth. What happened to Leo?"

He checked the living room windows and then glanced at the glassed-in breezeway, watching the moonlight for signs of darting shadows. Nothing but ancient cypress knees shooting up out of the still lake, and tall silent cypress trees guarding the mysteries of the darkness. But there were plenty of hiding places in this vast swampland.

"Look," he said, "I'm calling the locals. I get in enough

hot water without breaking the rules. I'll talk to them if you don't want to."

She finally nodded. "You're right. The sheriff will come and tell me there isn't much they can do."

He made the call and while they waited, he wondered why he'd decided to take on this task. The money was good and would help him be one step closer to getting out of this business.

He watched out the window, thinking she was probably right. No one was out there now.

Marco turned back to find her standing at the kitchen counter, one lone tear slipping down her cheek.

"He got sick, but he didn't tell anyone," he explained. "That's what the housekeeper and the lawyer told me."

"Leo sick?" She shook her head, wiped away the tear and stared down at the wooden counter. "Leo was as strong as an ox and always healthy."

"Apparently, it came on suddenly and he went down quick. They buried him a day or so after he died. I tried to find you."

"Rosa? Are she and Alan still there?"

"Yes." Alan and Rosa Mercer had been on the ranch for decades. They were upset about Leo Colón's death. "They're shocked and grieving."

"She'll tell me the truth."

"She's a good woman," he said. "She and Alan are taking care of things until you can get back to San Antonio."

"I can't go back there. I have no reason to go back there."

The way she'd said that with such conviction told him she wasn't gonna go easily. Her defiance stifled the room.

Marco stood across from her, his hands on the counter. "I'm here to say you do have a reason. You've inherited the ranch."

She sank down on a bar stool. "What?"

"That's why I've been looking for you," he said. "Leo died and Mr. Chastain called me right after the funeral. No one could locate you, but Mr. Chastain made it clear you need to get back to the Rio Rojo Ranch. He needs someone to take over."

Before they could finish the conversation, a sheriff's car pulled up. Marco whirled toward the door. "They'll want to talk to you."

"Okay, let's get it over with."

After they'd both given their statements to the stern sheriff's deputy, the man walked around the property and came back to tell him he'd found nothing. "Let me know if they come back."

Now Marco stood watching the dark woods. "Well, you were right. I guess hearing gunshots isn't unusual in these woods."

"More during hunting season," she said from the couch. "But we did report it, and he did promise to drive around and look for anyone suspicious."

Amelia got up and started making coffee. "I inherited the Triple R? Is this some kind of a joke?"

"No. It's real. Do you think I'd go creeping around in a swamp just for fun?"

She hit the brew button on the coffeepot and whirled to stare at him. "Are you going to hold a gun to my head and make me go back?"

"No," he replied, thinking this one was tough. "I was hoping you'd just hurry and hop in my truck."

She pulled her robe tight and reworked the sash, her

silver bracelet dancing down her arm in a quick sparkle. "I'm not prepared for this."

"Look, if you're worried about whoever is after you—"

"—you'll what? Protect me? Escort me back? Help me? I can handle getting there, but I can't handle being there."

He studied her, taking in the hair, the eyes, the little star-like scar on her left cheek, the freckles and what looked like a solid fear. Not about being shot at. A fear of going home, of facing whatever had scared her away. Marco knew that kind of fear. He'd left home years ago. But now that his father had died, he had a chance to make things better with the property he'd inherited.

"Are you saying you don't want the ranch?"

"No, I'm saying I don't want what comes with the ranch."

She turned and found two mugs. "Now let me see if I can round up a steak and some eggs."

Amelia cooked the steak and scrambled the eggs, her mind numb to the fact that a good-looking PI sat at her kitchen counter with a bottle of habanero sauce close by his fork.

After she'd cooked, she turned and handed him the plate of food and then poured him and herself a cup of coffee. "You never did show me your credentials, but you did save me from a bullet. So there's that."

He handed her his wallet and started eating his food. "Thank you. See for yourself."

She opened the wallet and studied his PI license. Looked authentic enough with the Lone Star flag in the left corner, just over his mug shot, and his name and signature clearly where they needed to be. And what kind of criminal would ask a woman to cook for him? This man was the real deal, which meant he'd want to finish what he started.

"I think you're legit," she said. "You could have easily killed me and taken my vast fortune by now."

He gave her a tight-lipped smile. "Excuse me, but your vast fortune is waiting at the ranch."

She sat down. "I'm still in shock about that."

He cut a big chunk of steak and chewed on it, his eyes on her. "I take it you and Leo were close."

She nodded. "But he's not really my uncle. My parents died in a car accident when I was fifteen. Leo and his wife, Siri, took me in and raised me from there. They never had children, so—"

"So you feel like their daughter?"

She didn't acknowledge that question. "Siri died three years ago. I had moved here by then, but I went back for her funeral. I'm—I was a photographer. Traveled a lot. I still do freelance work locally."

She stopped, staring at the bottle of sauce.

"But?"

"My fiancé was killed four years ago, a few weeks after we'd returned from a trip to Haiti. That night, he'd been to visit me at the ranch and his truck ran off the road, hit a tree and exploded."

Marco stopped eating. "Wow. So you lost your aunt and your fiancé close together, after losing your parents when you were young."

She nodded, holding back the memories of that horrible time. "After Siri's funeral, I left, and I never went back. Too painful. Too much I didn't understand."

"Meaning?"

"Meaning I don't want to talk about it, and I don't want that ranch."

"Look, I get you've lost a lot of people you love, but the ranch is yours. You're the only one listed on the will. It'll take a while for it to clear probate, but you own the place and that requires a lot of responsibility. You could always sell it."

"I'd never sell the Triple R."

"Then what do you plan to do with it?"

She put her elbows on the counter and placed her chin against her folded hands. "I have no idea."

He finished his meal and pushed the plate away. "I think you need to go and claim it at least. The Mercers are holding things together, but they loved your uncle. They need to see a friendly face."

"I'll have to think about this," she said. "I don't travel much since…since Daniel died. I still take photos, but I do landscapes and still life pictures. Mostly of this lake and the piney woods all over the countryside."

He glanced around at the walls covered in photos of the lake. And a few of a young Amelia with a man, a tropical jungle in the background. Daniel? "And you're good at it, obviously."

"I was." She shrugged, her gaze moving over the photos. "I just don't travel much."

"Are you afraid?"

"Of traveling?"

She nodded. "I have some newly developed phobias. My parents died in a car accident and so did my fiancé. After Daniel died, I limited my travels to places I can get to easily." She shrugged. "Around here, on foot or a bicycle can get me to town and back. I'm not scared of being in a vehicle. It's the memories that hit me when I crank a car."

He absorbed that information, thinking she was much too brave to use not being able to travel as an excuse. But he knew firsthand, memories could bring a man crashing to his knees. "I'll drive you to San Antonio."

She cleaned up the dishes and whirled to stare at him. "Look, thank you for letting me know about Uncle Leo. I'll need to call Samuel to verify all of this, but I have to process Leo's death and everything else you've told me. You don't want to stay through all that."

She went around checking doors and windows while he stood and watched the quiet panic settling over her like a lake fog.

"I'm not going anywhere," he replied, his coffee mug in his hand. "Someone tried to shoot you tonight, Amelia. I'm guessing that someone might want the Rio Rojo Ranch a lot more than you do. Your uncle's death makes me wonder if something's up. What if he didn't die of natural causes? So that means, where you go, I go. At least until we can figure this all out."

TWO

Amelia held up her hand, palm out in a hard no. "You can't stay here and follow me around twenty-four-seven," she said. "I'll handle this myself, as in, without you. You said Leo had been ill for a while."

Marco held his hand up just as she'd done. "I did report that, but with so many people around you dying, I'm seeing red flags everywhere. I promised Mr. Chastain I'd find you and bring you to San Antonio. I haven't finished the job and I want to finish so I can get paid and get on with my life."

Unlike her, he had land lying fallow and he couldn't wait to get back to that land and build a new home—his home—on the spot where he'd grown up. And he'd like to do it before any more developers tried to swoop in and turn it into a subdivision. He'd had enough offers to give him a comfortable income for the rest of his life. But he wasn't ready to sell out just yet.

"I'll pay you here and now." She reached into a drawer and pulled out a checkbook. "Name your price?"

"Oh, I see," he countered. "So you're one of those kinds?"

"Excuse me?"

"You pay people off to get your way."

"No, only the people who are *in* my way."

"I don't want your money. Chastain is paying me more than enough. But I need to get you to the ranch, and that's what I plan to do. Once I deliver you, I'm done."

He prayed she'd cooperate. Because he had long ago run out of prayers, and he really needed this one to work. If he could convince this woman to go and get this all settled, he'd have enough money to finally re-build everything his useless daddy had ruined. Not that he was hurting for money, but he would like to move out of the city. Traffic jams and sirens and too many people racing for the affluence they thought they had to have. Been there, tried that, lost the woman he thought he'd loved.

Amelia folded her arms in a protective gesture, the intricate bracelet shining like a protective shield. "I told you, I don't think I can go back there."

"Not even for a week, just to get all the paperwork filed and the deed done, to reassure Rosa and Alan that they won't be out of a job?"

"They'll never be out of a job."

"Then prove it to them. Show up and set this straight, so we can all get on with our lives."

She came around the counter and glared at him. "You can sleep on the couch tonight, but tomorrow I want you gone. I'll decide what's best for the Triple R. And I can do that from here and over the phone." Then she added, "Meantime, I'll call Samuel myself and tell him to pay you, that you've done your job. You've found me. And I'll get him to verify all of this. Because I still find it difficult to believe."

"That Leo died? Or that he left the ranch to you?"

"Both." She threw him a pillow and blanket and pointed to the bathroom next to the living area. Then she picked up her rifle and headed through the breezeway. "Good night, Marco."

Marco watched her go, then he checked the doors and windows again. She didn't have a security system, so apparently her rifle went where she went. But the doors were sturdy, and the windows had little stickers rating them for high impact. The cabin was rustic, but modern, a real home that had been carefully decorated with beautiful paintings of Texas landscapes, bluebonnets and the aged cypress trees on the lake.

He took in the perimeters—the big kitchen and comfortable den with a fireplace, the glassed breezeway designed with soft leather chairs and shelves of books underneath the windows, and down the hallway, her bedroom and probably another bath. An exit door out from the kitchen, where a large covered deck showed a moonlit view of the lake. The front door across from where he'd be sleeping tonight locked and deadbolted.

So why did he feel so exposed? This case had been iffy from the get-go. Chastain's cryptic requests and the amount of money he offered only added to the fuel. But Marco's sense of duty harked back to his two tours of duty as an Army Ranger in Afghanistan.

He always finished what he started. But this case had been surprising all around. Especially now, with a beautiful, reclusive woman to deal with. A woman somebody had tried to kill.

The shooter could still be out there, waiting for the right moment to try again. But who? No way anyone could have tracked him here. He always covered his tracks. Besides, who had it in for him or her? Maybe someone here on the lake? He could see Amelia Garcia making someone mad, but why shoot at her?

That didn't make sense. Amelia would have mentioned someone having it in for her, or maybe not, her being all prickly and stone-faced and stubborn. And pretty. The woman was pretty in that wild-child, bohemian way, but he couldn't get a read on her. Couldn't decide if she'd do what she needed to do or kick him to the curb. Something held her back and that something had to be the reason she was hiding out here. Did she know already who had come to do her in?

He decided he'd sleep with his boots on, with his gun ready and one eye open, just in case. Just another day at the office.

He fluffed the plaid pillow, threw the blanket across his legs and closed his eyes, a bone-deep weariness coming over him. The fall weather had become a welcome relief, but he didn't want to be pushed out in the cold tonight. He just needed a few minutes of shut-eye. When he woke suddenly three hours later, the cabin was on fire.

She was having the same dream. The one where she heard the horrible screeching of tires, and the squeal of grinding, crashing metal followed by a boom that rocked the house and then the sound of an explosion. Then the shouts, the sirens, the sheriff at the door, telling Leo and her that Daniel's truck had hit a tree after leaving the drive to their house.

On their land. Just around the curve.

Daniel, the love of her life who'd lived next to their property on his own ranch, the man she'd loved since high school, now gone in a flaming explosion that had left his truck and the trees on fire.

Amelia woke screaming and drenched with a cold sweat. She blinked, pushed at her hair, then smelled the same acrid odor she'd smelled that night. Smoke and fire!

In her cabin.

She jumped up, grabbing at clothes and shoes, and out of habit, searching for her camera bag and her tote. Then she heard a shout outside her door.

"Amelia, wake up."

Who?

Marco Landon, the private investigator. Marco was here, and the cabin was on fire. A shooter earlier and now this. Someone was after her.

She tried to call out, but still weak from the dream, she couldn't find her voice or her breath. She didn't want to pass out. She had to get out of here.

"Amelia?"

The locked door to her room crashed open and he came toward her, grabbed her tote and camera bag out of her hands, then lifted her up and into his arms, shielding her face as he ran back through the breezeway and hurried toward the only exit not on fire. But the door to the back deck was jammed. Marco couldn't get it to budge.

"The breezeway," she said on a hoarse note. "A lock on the left. A hidden latch on the last window toward the lake."

Marco hurried to the breezeway, smoke and flames chasing him. He glanced to the left as she'd told him. Then he moved to the last window before her bedroom. "Here?"

She nodded. "Hit the latch."

He found the small hidden latch and lifted the lever. The window swung open. Dropping her onto the deck, he came out after her and then dragged her toward the water.

Once he had her off the deck and down by the dock, he dropped to his knees and set her on the cool, damp grass.

"Are you okay?" he asked, searching her face.

She nodded. "My cabin."

"I called the fire department. On the way."

"My photos, my paintings."

"I've got your camera bag and purse," he said, showing her where he'd slung them over his back.

Amelia glanced at the black camera bag and the buttery leather tote that went with her everywhere. Then she started laughing.

Marco held her arms. "You're going into shock."

She couldn't stop laughing. "You just look so funny with all my stuff hanging on your back. And you managed to drag me out with all that, too."

He touched his hands to her face. "You're in shock. Are you going to pass out on me?"

She shook her head, her laughter turning to tears. "No, and I'm not going to cry either. I mean it."

He tugged her close. "I know you mean it, but help is on the way and I'm here."

Amelia fell into his arms, not sure why she needed to be held. But it had been so long, and she'd forgotten how to touch, how to love, how to hope, how to pray. She'd sealed herself off from the world, her heart broken and burned, and now someone had come to help her. So she cried, because that someone was asking her to do the one thing she'd never wanted.

To go back to Rio Rojo Ranch.

Only now, she had no other choice. Her home here was going up in flames.

They hid in the woods until the authorities arrived, but the cabin was halfway gone by then. Marco had watched for shadows but saw none. Was someone out there watching, making sure Amelia didn't survive? Could someone be watching them now and waiting to make the next move?

What if he'd left earlier? Amelia might be dead by now.

"Any hope of rebuilding?" Marco asked one of the firefighters who hurried by.

"Yep, if someone has the blueprints. This will need to be torn down. Best to get the insurance money to build a new cabin."

Marco nodded, then went to talk to the sheriff. He showed his credentials. Then he took the sheriff to where Amelia sat on an old swing. "Amelia, the sheriff needs our statements."

She lifted her head. "I gave a statement to one of your deputies earlier. He didn't seem all that worried."

"Ma'am, do you know what started the fire?"

"No," she said, her tone full of numbness and shock. "I was in my room asleep. But someone did shoot at us earlier."

The sheriff's bullish head came up. "I'll check on that report. We did have a deputy riding through here every thirty minutes. Humor me, though, and tell me everything again."

"After I arrived," Marco said, "we were…talking on the porch and someone fired two shots at us. You might find a bullet in the porch post to the left of the door. Or what's left of the porch post."

"Uh-huh." The man glanced at Amelia. "You got enemies, Miss Garcia?"

"None that I know of."

"We were kind of surprised," Marco explained. "I got her inside and checked the doors and windows. We got involved in why I came here. But we did decide to report the shooter." He named the deputy who'd shown up earlier. "He looked around but didn't find anyone."

The older gray-haired sheriff looked doubtful. "I see. Explain again why you're here, Mr. Landon?"

"I was looking for Miss Garcia," Marcus said. "Her uncle passed away and his lawyer wanted her to know."

The burly sheriff glanced from one to the other. "Interesting." Then he asked, "You two an item?"

"What? Us?" Amelia stood up. "I don't see how that has anything to do with what happened tonight. This man came to find me, and someone must have followed him to shoot at us."

The sheriff jumped right on that theory. "So you brought trouble to our quiet little town?"

"No, I didn't," Marco replied, that bone-weary tiredness making him ornery. "I did my job, and I covered my tracks, but I do believe someone is out to harm Miss Garcia. So maybe you should do your job, too?"

"Do you believe this man is on your side?" the sheriff asked Amelia.

She glanced at Marco and then back to the sheriff. "I know he's on my side. He saved my life twice tonight." Then she turned to look at the remnants of her home. "If you've got enough information, Sheriff, I have to make arrangements and find somewhere to stay." Glancing at Marco, then back to the sheriff, she added, "I'll give you my uncle's address in San Antonio. We were planning to go there first thing this morning so I can take care of his estate."

Marco nodded and stayed silent. The choice had been made for her, and now for him, too. Someone had forced her hand. To make sure she'd show up at Rio Rojo Ranch, or to make sure she died before she ever got there?

He'd like to know the answer to that question.

THREE

Six hours later, Marco drove his Chevy along the county line road toward the Rio Rojo, or as Amelia had called it, the Triple R. She'd put up a fight about him driving her here.

"I can get myself to the ranch," she'd huffed once he told her they needed to leave Wildflower while it was still dark out.

"On what? Your bicycle?"

"My bike is a Harley," she'd explained after they'd watched the firefighter put out the last embers of the fire.

"Was it parked in that little shed by the back door?"

She glanced around, then shook her head. "It was."

"Amelia, that went up right after the firefighters arrived. I think your bike is toast, and even if you could ride it to San Antonio in the middle of the night, that would be too dangerous. You'd be an easy target on a motorcycle."

"Then I guess I'm stuck with you," she'd retorted, tugging at the old boots she'd found stored away in what was left of her closet. They were soggy on the outside but fairly comfortable, she'd insisted. She'd also grabbed a few things that hadn't melted or burned, but for the most part her home was gone.

After they'd checked everything and found nothing left to save, she'd talked to the sheriff about looters.

"We'll keep an eye out until you get back." Then he warned them to alert him if anything else happened. "You might be in trouble, Miss Garcia. So don't take this lightly."

Amelia grabbed what little she had left. "I'm taking this very seriously, Sheriff, I can assure you."

Now she sat tense and silent, her eyes straight ahead. The sun peeked through the trees to the west, a muted golden-pink awakening that gave the facade of a perfect morning. Marco thought she'd sleep, but she didn't. Nor did she talk all that much. He'd offered her food and drink, but she'd only sipped the bottled water he had in the truck.

"Hey, you okay over there?"

She shifted and nodded. Then she asked, "Why did you become a private investigator?"

Surprised at that train of thought, he glanced over at her, seeing her in the shimmer of the sun's wink. Her hair glistened, but her eyes filled with dread and expectation. She needed a distraction. "I don't know. Kind of stumbled into it after a few bad runs."

"I guess you catch a lot of people doing a lot of bad things, right?"

"I've surveilled a few in my life, yes. Some are meaner than a snake, and some have just been betrayed one time too many. I see couples break up after one had an affair, or people reunited, after they've been apart a long time."

"One of them could be after you. One of the bad ones, I mean. Someone you spied on and reported on."

"I don't think this is about me."

"Well, where did you grow up?"

"Oh, so you want my life history—after hours of giving me the stink-eye?"

"Did I do that?"

"Several times."

"I'd like to know more about you." She rearranged herself, but still held the tense attitude, her face framed in a perpetual frown. "I mean you did spend the night in my house."

"Okay, here's the rundown. I grew up on a small ranch near Austin. But when I was a teenager, we almost lost the ranch, but we all got jobs to pay the mortgage—me, my mom and even my drunkard dad. We barely managed to hold on, but we did somehow. I own it now, but it's fallow land, no cattle, not even a house. Some construction company wants to build a subdivision there, but I'm holding out as long as I can. I want to rebuild and make something of the old place."

She gave him a look that held a tad of respect and understanding. "So you left as soon as you could, I mean, after your folks and you held on to the place?"

"No, not for a while. I had to stay and help my mom. My daddy died of a heart attack—stress can do that to a man. Especially a man who drank too much, messed up his liver and didn't care about providing for his family." Shaking his head, he said, "In the end, he did try. But it was too late. He wasted away into nothing. I pray I won't turn out like him."

"You obviously haven't, Marco. You seem focused and good at what you do."

"Yep, but the money doesn't come easy."

"I'm sorry. So is your mother still there?"

"We lived in a small apartment for a while, since the house was a mess, and the land was even worse." He shrugged. "Then her brother found us and took us in. That's when I left and joined the Army. He and I clashed on just about everything. My mom has her own place now, a small apartment on the outskirts of Austin. She works in a hospital cafeteria. She's doing good." And he made sure she had money to tide her over.

"You still haven't told me about you."

"I served the Army Rangers, after joining up and training at Fort Benning, Georgia. Did two tours."

Amelia sat up straight and stared over at him. "Well, that explains a lot."

"Yeah, a lot is what it became."

Marco decided to skip over the details of his military background. No need for her to know too much about him or his bad memories. He'd be gone soon enough. "After I returned from my last tour of duty, I moved from job to job and got in trouble until a nice police officer took me under his wing. He worked with a lot of PIs, and I got interested, so I took the necessary courses and training to get my license. And here we are, six years later."

"You don't like to talk about yourself, right?"

"I see no need. I don't owe my clients any explanations."

"I'm not your client."

"No, you're not. Even more reason to keep my private life private."

"While you know everything about mine."

"Yep."

She glanced at the road signs, then sat up straight. "We're almost there."

And just like that, she changed the subject. Into silence.

"Why is it so hard?" he asked, needing to know.

She wrapped the jacket he'd loaned her around her stomach. "I can't talk about it. I don't want to be here, accepting that yet another person I love has died."

Marco nodded and regretted snapping at her. "I'm sorry, Amelia."

"Yeah, me, too."

Then she turned and stared out at the countryside.

Marco didn't get emotionally involved with his clients. Usually he did his job, got the right information to the right people, took his money and left. He didn't like messy, and he tried to keep things tidy and done. His childhood had been chaos, so now he liked to keep things on track. And he did not get involved with clients. Or the people he sometimes had to find.

But this one was different, tough as nails but vulnerable, too. Something she didn't want the world to see. Only he'd seen it, and she resented that. She was a lot like him, keeping her secrets to herself.

He turned the truck to the left and saw the gate to the ranch. It was sparse and understated compared with most Texas ranch entrances. A long solid beam of what looked like oak wood went across the top and two similar beams held it up on both sides.

The name of the ranch was carved in the crossbeam with the smaller carving of Triple R underneath it. Wrought iron gates protected the perimeters of the main property, but the ranch extended for a thousand acres as far as the eye could see. Marco pulled his truck up to the intercom and waited for someone to speak.

"Yes," came a voice surrounded by static.

"Marco Landon. I have Amelia Garcia with me."

The gate swung open. And then slowly closed behind them.

Amelia seemed to curl into the passenger side of the truck, her expression pinched with agony, her eyes glued to the road ahead. "I don't think I can do this, Marco."

Sensing a panic attack, he grabbed her hand. "You're not alone here. I'll stay. I'm going wherever you go until we get to the bottom of what happened last night."

"I'm not the one who hired you."

"No, but you're the one I'm going to protect."

"I can protect myself."

"Amelia, you don't look so sure about that. You don't have to be brave with me. You were shot at, you lost your home and you found out the man who raised you is dead. You're entitled to a meltdown."

"I don't do drama."

Marco found that hard to believe. His ex-girlfriend had perfected the art of dramatic fits—in public. He needed to remember that and get Amelia inside and get his money in his pocket. He refused to deal with any woman who didn't know what she really wanted. "Maybe a good fit is what you need."

She gave him a hard stare. "I can't have a meltdown, or a hissy fit, or any kind of fit. If I truly own this place now, I have to be strong for everyone. For Leo and Siri and the memories I have of them, and for Daniel. Even for my own parents. I have to make this work, Marco. For their sakes."

Marco stopped the truck midway to the imposing stone-and-wood house that sat long and lofty at the end of the tree-lined drive. "Then I'm staying here until you think you've got it all under control. Someone doesn't want you here, Amelia. We need to find out who that someone is."

Amelia took in the grandeur of the Rio Rojo. This place had always taken her breath away, but now it made her eyes get misty. Memories floated to the surface of her emotions, stirring up the old anxiety and angst. She'd loved this place the first time her parents had brought her here and now, she missed it with the intensity of missing a piece of her heart.

The heavy rounded stones from the foundation reached to meet the solid wood of the twists and angles of the house. Built as a true hacienda, it was shaped in a wide U style that held a flower-infused courtyard with a trickling fountain that always lulled her to sleep at night. Back when she could sleep.

"It hasn't changed much," she said now. "They keep it painted and pretty, always have updated it as the years move on. But this house was built solid in the early part of last century so it's well over a hundred years old."

"It holds its secrets, I reckon."

"It does. Too many secrets."

"Don't we all have secrets?" he asked, ready to get her inside, where Samuel Chastain was probably waiting. He wouldn't feel guilty about leaving her with this mess. Not his mess to deal with, but then he'd told her he was sticking around until she had some answers. Samuel would take care of her once this was over. He hoped.

"I'm not as much worried about who's after me as I am the memories of this place and what I'll have to go through over the next few days. I don't know if I can ever live here."

"Is it that bad?"

"I love the Triple R, but I was forced to live here when I had no one else, no other place to go. Leo was my godfather and the obvious choice. Siri was so good to me. I was a teenager, Marco. So confused and alone. But they welcomed me and pampered me, even offered to adopt me. But I wanted to keep my name and my heritage. I wanted to remember my parents and their struggles."

"I get that."

"I think you might," she said. "My parents worked here, you see. Same as the Mercers. My daddy was the ranch foreman, and my mother was an assistant to Siri—an artist. The paintings I lost last night came from Siri and my mother."

"Wow." Surprise colored his dark eyes. "I'm sorry."

"Well, that's life. Now I have to go in there and figure all of this out."

"And you resent my part in this."

"I resent that this had to happen. I was content in my little cabin. I had it built to my specifications and I've lived there for close to six years. Now it's gone. Thankfully, I have my work stored in an electronic cloud somewhere. I can bring up most of my photos. But those paintings were priceless."

"You mean money-wise?"

"I mean emotional-wise to me. But yes, they were valuable, too."

"You have a lot to work through. Were they insured?"

"Yes, only because Leo made sure of that."

"I know that won't soothe your pain, but that is something."

"I don't care. I'd rather have my life back the way it was before you darkened my door." Then she relented.

"I'm sorry. You've helped me and I do appreciate that. This is just all too much."

He nodded and opened the truck door. "Then let's get on this so I can leave the way I came."

"I'm not saying I want you to leave," she amended, her heart doing strange things each time she looked into those deep brown eyes. "I'm saying I wish you didn't have such an awful reason to find me."

Had she just said that? She was too stressed to watch her words. "I'm sorry. I need to think this through and say a lot of prayers for wisdom and for our safety. All of our safety."

"I wish we'd met under different circumstances, too," he replied, his tone husky and hushed. "I think in spite of you being so prickly, we could have hit it off. Now I can see that's not possible."

He got out and came around to open the door for her. Amelia sat shocked at his declaration. He was here for a purpose and that included getting her here, only so he'd get his salary and then he'd be gone.

One more person out of her life.

She slid out of the truck, dreading every minute she'd have to spend here. This house held all of her hopes and dreams and also all of her woes and failures, and her losses.

How could she ever survive this? Amelia silently asked God to guide her. Her mother had shown her faith and Siri and Leo had carried on that tradition. Sometimes she thought her faith was the only true cornerstone of her life.

Marco's gaze moved over her. "Hey, before we go in, I hope you figure things out." He brushed his hand over his jacket and glanced back at the road out.

Amelia appreciated him, but she could see he wanted to be gone. "Thank you." He'd told her enough about his past to show he had a lot of torment hiding behind those dark eyes. Too much for her to deal with right now.

Marco held a hand against the small of her back as they reached the front door. But when they heard a spine-chilling scream from inside, they looked at each other and hurried. Marcus didn't bother knocking, but the door wasn't locked so he rushed inside, Amelia right behind him, her hand holding on to his arm, her mind whirling with what they might find.

Apparently, trouble had followed them to the Triple R.

FOUR

Rosa Mercer stood in the massive kitchen to the right of the hallway with her hands to her face, her husband, Alan, holding her with an arm around her shoulder.

Marco rushed through the arched entry to the kitchen, his weapon ready. "What happened?"

Alan and Rosa turned and when Rosa saw Amelia, she rushed into her arms. "I'm so glad you're home."

Amelia hugged the petite woman and said, "I'm here. What just happened?"

Alan lowered his gaze, then glanced at Marco. "She thought she saw Daniel."

Amelia stepped back, shock making her go pale. "Daniel? That… That can't be."

"I told her that," Alan said. "It's been a few rough weeks. I think we're all exhausted."

"I saw him in the courtyard," Rosa said, her dark eyes misting over. Then she shook her head. "Maybe I just miss him all over again now that Leo's gone."

Marco instinctively went toward the two glass doors that opened out onto a lush courtyard full of cacti, mesquite trees and blooming vines with a long table and matching set of chairs centered by a flowing foundation.

"Describe the person you saw," Marco said to Rosa.

Rosa glanced to her husband. "You didn't see him?"

"No. But I believe you saw someone."

Rosa nodded. "*Si.* He had dark blond hair like Daniel and the same eyes, but his face was different." She shrugged. "A man was there, a man who could have been Daniel…"

"Except what?" Amelia asked, her heart being pierced with a thousand arrows of agony.

"He looked evil," Rosa said, her hand to her mouth again. "Evil."

Marco opened the doors and went out. Then he came back inside. "Nothing. The back gate wasn't locked, but it was shut. Maybe it was one of the ranch hands?"

"They usually use the back kitchen door," Alan said. "And they knock first." Shrugging, he added, "We know their faces, Marco. It couldn't have been a worker."

Amelia ignored Marco's pointed stare and pulled out a chunky chair, then sank down against the long cypress wood dining table. She didn't want memories of Daniel to override Leo's death. That would be too much. "Grief can make us imagine strange things. I wish every day that Daniel was still alive. And now I can't believe Uncle Leo is gone. I'm sorry I wasn't here, Rosa."

Rosa shook her head. "He was doing fine and then, he just went downhill so quickly once it started."

"Do you know what caused his death?" Amelia asked.

Marco had eyes on Rosa. Rosa looked up at him but said nothing. Then she wiped her face and turned back to Amelia. "I'm sorry, but we don't know yet. Let me get you both some food. Mr. Chastain is on his way."

Amelia stood. "I can help."

"No, no." Rosa's smile widened. "I have made all of your favorites, *bonita*. Tamales, *bife* tacos and flan for a late lunch. I have freshly made cinnamon rolls for breakfast, just the way you like them."

Amelia's stomach roiled. She was hungry but not sure she could eat a bite. "Maybe I'll just freshen up first."

"Your room is clean and ready," Alan said. Then he touched her arm. "Amelia, we're so sorry about Leo. You know I loved him like a brother. He always said we were part of the family."

Rosa shook her head. "He was so good to us, always."

"I loved him, too," she said, hugging Alan. "I want to hear everything after we eat." She started toward the long hallway to the other side of the house.

"I'll go with you," Marco said. "Just to check."

Rosa and Alan both looked confused. "Just in case of what?" Alan asked.

"If that intruder is still lurking about."

Amelia gave Marco a warning look. "And just in case I try to run away," she said with a laugh. "But I'm here now and I'm not going anywhere soon."

"Neither am I," Marco told the anxious couple. Then he gave them his own warning glance.

Alan picked up on things. "Marco, we have a guest suite on the other side of the house if you feel the need to stay a few days."

"I might take you up on that offer," he said as he moved to follow Amelia. "We'll see how things go."

Alan nodded his understanding, then turned to help his wife.

Marco had to walk fast to keep up with Amelia. She sure didn't like anyone hovering over her. She'd wrapped herself up in grief and couldn't see beyond her broken heart.

"Hey," he said, grabbing her arm when she stopped at a corner room, "are you okay?"

"You know I'm not okay. I lost my parents, then Daniel and Siri, and now Uncle Leo, then last night I lost my home and now I'm back here. I had made myself a good life, a quiet life, before you came to see me. Now, my life has changed literally overnight. So I'm a little bitter about things."

"I'm sorry for that and for your grief," he said, letting out a breath, "but have you stopped to think about how things could have turned out if I hadn't showed up?"

She opened the heavy wooden door and motioned him inside. "You're right. I could be dead and while I'm forever grateful, I find it strange that whoever tried to gun me down showed up when you did. I'm not saying you were involved. Just wondering how that happened."

Marco took in the room, checking for entryways. Then he came back and put a finger to his lips. In a soft whisper, he said, "It happened because someone knows your uncle died, and that someone probably has this place bugged. Maybe not this room, but the main rooms. I'll need to check."

To prove that point, he ran his hands over the lamps and opened the nightstands, and even checked under the bed. He studied the air-conditioning vents but couldn't reach them without a ladder.

Motioning to the en suite bath, he followed her in the luxurious room and checked every nook and corner there before turning on the water as loud and fast as it would go. The room was rectangular and big, with high windows that would allow sunlight and moonlight, too narrow for a human to crawl through.

Leaning close again, he whispered, "I'm still wondering about Chastain. What his angle is."

Amelia's eyes flared with disbelief when she hissed a return whisper. "He's Leo's lawyer and best friend. You can mark him off your list and remember he's paying your salary."

"Yes, and he demanded updates on my search with every step. He'd be able to track me if he wanted to. Or have someone track me. I'll make sure my truck doesn't have a bug on it."

She shook her head and backed away from his whispers. "None of this makes any sense."

"Well, until it does, consider everyone a suspect." Then he waved one hand in the air, turned off the water and took her back to the other room. "This is a big bedroom—no, make that a suite."

The room had a cozy sitting area with two matching light blue leather chairs and a paned sliding door out to the courtyard. He moved over to check that door. Locked up tight, but no security measures beyond that. Then he checked the walk-in closet and noticed the boots, jeans and other clothing she must have left behind.

Amelia sank down in one of the chairs. "Are you finished checking for the monsters under the bed?"

He whirled and glared at her. "The monsters could be out in that courtyard."

Amelia got up and stared him down. "The monsters are in my head, Marco. Daniel? Rosa thought she saw him. I have to live with his death every day of my life. Before that, it was my parents, and then Siri. Now,

Leo. Everyone I've ever loved has left me, and Rosa is scared she's seeing ghosts."

"What if she really did see someone out there?"

"I can't…go there right now."

"We need to go there. Rosa seemed sure she'd seen a man in the courtyard. I believe her."

Amelia stopped, held a hand to her mouth. "No, I need to get it together right now, and I can't do that with you standing there making all these suggestions and assumptions."

"Amelia…?"

"No. You don't know me well enough to be my friend. You know way too much already, though, information you found by asking around, by going deep online. I need some time alone, to absorb all of this, to think, to figure out what happens next. After that, I could sleep for a week, but I don't have that luxury."

"Do you want me to take my money and leave?"

She was about to say something when they heard a knock on the door. "Amelia, Samuel Chastain is here," Alan called out.

"I'll be there soon," she said, her right hand grabbing at her hair. "Go, Marco, talk to him while I get a quick shower and find some clean clothes."

Marco lifted a hand, then dropped it. He wanted to help this woman, wanted to keep her safe. Feelings he'd never had for a client before, and feelings he needed to end right now.

She was pricklier than any cactus he'd ever come across and as about as stubborn as a wild mustang.

Although Amelia wasn't the person who'd hired him, she was the person someone wanted dead, and thankful that he'd found her in time, he wouldn't leave until he knew she'd be safe.

"You think about my question," he said as he headed for the door. "I can leave at any time, or I can stay and help figure this out. It's your call."

Amelia didn't say a word. She just stared at the floor, her arms crossed in a protective shield against her heart.

He left her like that and then, tired and frustrated, headed to the other side of this enormous house, his mind still on the man Rosa thought she'd seen out there.

Daniel couldn't have been that man, but Marco believed Rosa had seen someone out there. Someone who wanted Amelia dead.

Amelia hurried to get dressed. After finding some jeans and a light sweater she'd left in the closet, she threw on her boots and dried her hair with the old drier in the bathroom closet, leaving it a little damp in her haste. Rosa had kept her room almost the way she'd left it, so she at least had clothes. And Rosa had also put a basket of good-smelling toiletries in the bathroom. Amelia would thank her friend later.

Finding her bracelet, she slid the latch through the round hook, making sure it was secure. This bracelet had been a gift from Leo, but Daniel had given her several of the charms on it. Siri had added a few here and there. Now it held special memories from all of them. Each time the charms clinked and tinkled, she thought of all the people she'd lost.

Now she had someone after her.

Right now, she needed coffee and explanations.

When she heard voices in the huge den on the other side of the kitchen, she kept walking the long hallway.

Rosa had set out coffee and her famous cinnamon rolls on a side table. Amelia grabbed a cup and filled it with the rich brew Rosa kept stocked, then took a plated roll so she wouldn't hurt Rosa's feelings.

"There you are," Sam Chastain said as she entered the den. He looked as debonair as ever, his thick hair now completely white, his suit tailored to perfection.

Amelia set down her coffee and food and gave the white-haired lawyer a hug. "Samuel, thank you for letting me know about Leo. I mean, finding me to let me know."

Samuel gave her a long, sad stare. "And you were hard to find at that. I'm so sorry, darlin'. I sure wanted you to know, of course. But it was an urgent matter, too. We'll have a formal reading of the will whenever you're ready, but now you know why I sent Marco to find you."

Marco took a sip of coffee and motioned to her. "Why don't we sit down."

"Of course," Samuel said, waiting for Amelia.

She found her favorite chair, a soft paisley material with flowers twirling through the design. "I'm still in shock," she admitted. About so many things.

Taking in the room's massive fireplace and set of glass doors that gave a beautiful view of the pastures and the Chiquita River beyond, she decided this place hadn't changed much. But she had. She wouldn't back down on finding out the truth.

But she had to wonder how much Marco had told Samuel.

"So what were you two discussing?" she asked, hoping for some clues.

Marco finished his coffee. "I filled Samuel in on what happened at your place."

"I'm so sorry," Samuel said. "Rosa said you loved your new home. I agree with Marcus—he should stay here and help solve this problem. I can't believe someone tried to hurt you. You don't have to live looking over your shoulder all the time."

Surprised that Marco hadn't outright accused Samuel, she could only guess he hadn't been paid yet. "I told Marco he doesn't need to stay, but I would feel better if we retained him a while longer. I can't make any decisions when someone wants me dead."

Both men looked surprised, but Marco also looked relieved while Samuel looked shocked.

"The only decision you need to make," Samuel said, his hand waving in flourish, "is regarding Rio Rojo Ranch. Do you want to keep the Triple R going, Amelia? Or are you planning to sell out and move on?"

Amelia took a long sip of the rich coffee and then broke off a piece of warm cinnamon roll with her fork. After she'd enjoyed that small bite of bliss, she glanced from Samuel to Marco. "What I want right now is the truth. Samuel, do you have any idea who wants me dead and out of the way?"

Samuel had just taken a bite of his own roll, and now he started coughing. Marco got him some water and Amelia gave him a concerned look.

"I'm fine," he said. "Your question just threw me off a little bit. But you always were direct and to the point."

"I haven't changed," she said. "Only now I'm stronger and I need the truth. If you know more than you're saying, now is the time to confess all."

Marco gave her an inquisitive glance that held a touch of admiration. Then he glanced at Samuel. "You heard the lady. Do you know why anyone would want to do harm to Amelia?"

Samuel's gray eyes widened. "I...uh—"

Alan came into the room. "Amelia, we have a problem. Someone cut the fence in the north pasture. We got cattle running wild and not enough help to round them up."

Marco and Amelia both stood at the same time. "This can't be an accident," Marco said. "I can go check it out."

"We'll both go," she replied. "I still know how to ride a horse, and herd cattle." She took one last drink of her coffee. "And I'll bring my gun."

"You'll be exposed out there."

"I just hired you to protect me, so let's go."

Marco grunted and followed her out the door toward the stables. "I don't like this."

"You don't ride?"

"Horses? Yes, and I can round up cattle. But you shouldn't go out there."

"Technically, I own the ranch now, so technically, I'm the boss. And the boss always saddles up, cowboy. Lead, follow or get out of the way."

She spun like a top and headed toward the back door of the kitchen.

Marco grunted again. But he followed her.

FIVE

Once they were saddled up and riding out with several ranch hands, Marco caught up with her. She'd picked the meanest horse from the way the gelding kept throwing his mane back while he tried to show off.

"Buster is my horse," she'd said with a shrug as she'd hopped up on him. "Or at least he was. He remembers me."

"If you say so," Marco had replied. He'd been given a big roan, but a docile one. He could handle horses, but not horses and one mad, stubborn, tired woman, too. She'd shoot first and ask questions later.

"So what do you think about Samuel?" he asked as they trotted toward the pasture, the fall air crisp on his skin.

"I think he's doing his job."

"He looked surprised when you said I could stay."

"I was surprised about that myself. That and the fact that I'm willing to stay, too."

"Well, I'm glad we got that settled," he retorted. "Now let's find those cattle."

She tipped her hat and took off, Buster gleefully flying through the air, his hoofs slapping dirt up in dusty little puffs. Marco followed along with a half-dozen able hands, ready to round up the cattle and to find anyone who might be trespassing.

Probably the same man Rosa had seen in the court-yard. Someone was going full siege on this ranch. Maybe Amelia was right. Maybe this place only held bad memories. As beautiful and lush as this ranch was, it wore a melancholy facade that gave Marco a deep burn in his gut. Something wasn't right, but he'd find out what soon enough.

Once they reached the damaged fence, the ranch foreman who'd alerted them showed Amelia and Marco the cuts in the heavy barbed wire. Cut and stretched wide so cattle could run right through or be herded into a waiting trailer.

Ben Nesmith's smirk stayed solid against his leathery skin while he explained to Amelia about the fence. He looked to be in his early fifties, wrinkled from the sun and ornery by nature.

"Leo would have my hide about this," he told Amelia. "If you're taking over, you'll see what actually goes on around here. I've worked hard to keep things going, but it's getting tougher every day. A lot of things neglected, need fixing. Alan and Rosa don't bother to take care of anything much."

Amelia gave Marco a quick glance, then turned back to the man. Marco listened in while he scanned the countryside. The beauty of the place captured him, but the happenings around here made him wonder.

"Let's not discuss Alan and Rosa since the house and grounds are spotless and thriving," Amelia said to Nesmith. "As far as I know, since Leo died, you're in charge of the rest. One step at a time, and right now this broken fence is at the top of the list. I'm playing catch-up and I understand I'm a lot different from Uncle Leo. You all miss him, I'm sure. Well, I just learned last night that he died, so I've got lots of questions, first being—tell me what happened with this fence. Fence-cutting seems kind of old-school to me."

"It is old-school," Nesmith finally retorted, his tone harsh. "Because it's the easiest way to get a rancher fired up. We've got twenty head of cattle to round up. Good thing we hadn't sent the whole herd to this east pasture. But these heifers are still valuable. This is the simple part—someone cut the fence and now we got a mess on our hands."

Amelia put her hand on her hip. "You mean our cattle could be on a truck to the nearest cattle station?"

"Yes, and they'd be sold by nightfall," Nesmith replied.

"Okay, we need to alert the cattle stations within a hundred-mile radius and tell them to watch for any livestock with our brand," Amelia said. "I'll call Alan to do that while we're searching, and I'll follow up on it, too. And once we're done, I'll go over the layout of the pastures. We might need to rethink the ones near busy roadways, and we might consider varying our feed times. Then I'll need a list of anyone who has a set of keys or the security codes on the gates all over the ranch."

Marco turned to see Nesmith's response to that firm retort.

"Are you suggesting one of us did this?" Nesmith asked, his tone simmering on angry, while his eyes held a trace of admiration.

"I'm not suggesting anything yet," Amelia replied.

"I hope this was just a prank and we find our cattle. But I plan to thoroughly question all of you, one at a time, and alone."

Marco had been within hearing distance, searching for footprints around the cut fence, but now he stepped in and glared at the other man. "And me. I go where she goes."

Amelia didn't argue, so Marco kept talking. "We start on the ranch and work our way out. Those cattle are worth a lot of money, and everyone here knows that. Makes sense to me."

Nesmith snorted and waved a hand at Marco. "You don't even know this ranch."

"He's with me," Amelia said. "End of discussion."

Amelia turned to one of the workers who'd stayed behind to watch for strays. "After we return with the cattle, you make sure you get this fence mended, all right? If we don't return with cattle, this still needs to be fixed."

The young man looked to Ben Nesmith.

"Excuse me," Amelia said. "I'm asking you, so look at me, please."

The bashful man bobbed his head. "Yes, ma'am. We've got tools in the truck back there. Good thing we were checking fences today."

"That is a good thing," Amelia said, giving him a smile. "I'm depending on you, Tommy, is it?"

"Yes, ma'am." Tommy kept his eyes on her. "I'll take care of it."

"And Tommy, let any workers who aren't helping with the round-up meet back here this afternoon. I need to talk to each of you."

Nesmith nodded to the young man and Tommy took

off to the truck parked a few yards away by the lane. Then the aggravated foreman turned back to Amelia. "So you're really in charge now, I reckon. But you might want to remember, I've been in charge for a few years now. You didn't care one bit until you found out Leo had left this place to you."

"Hey, that's enough," Marco said. "She didn't want to come back here."

"Then why did she?"

Amelia held up her hand. "Listen, Ben, you're right. I left for my own reasons, and I was shocked to find out Leo had left the ranch to me. I'm only here to decide what to do about that and I haven't had much time to let it sink in."

"Well, you've brought trouble we don't need."

"I'm going to find out who's behind that trouble," she said. "But for now, I'm the boss. I've got a lot to think about and figure out. Leo died and someone is trying to get me out of the way. And if I find out it's someone on this ranch, that person will pay, get my drift?"

Nesmith's eyes flared with anger, but Marco shot him a warning glance. Shifting on his dusty boots, Nesmith nodded. "Sure, Miss Amelia. I understand perfectly. We'll get it all taken care of while you're trying to *figure things out*."

Marco glared at him again.

Amelia just nodded. "Okay, then drop the attitude and let's go find our cattle."

She swung up on her horse and headed out to catch up with the other riders. Marco shot Ben a glance. "You wouldn't have any idea who'd want her gone, would you?"

Nesmith snorted. "If I did, I wouldn't tell you. I'd

tell her. She's the boss." Then he tossed out, "But not for long."

"I wouldn't go around saying such if I were you," Marco retorted. "Everyone is a suspect, as I have to keep reminding people."

Then he got on his roan and took off, Nesmith coming up behind him. He planned to keep an eye on the foreman. Wouldn't be the first time an old rancher didn't like having a woman boss.

He didn't trust anyone on this ranch, but his gut told him this could be an inside job. A lot of people worked this huge ranch and any one of them could want a piece of it, or all of it. But the people after Amelia would have to had known about the will. And only a handful of people knew that. He planned to come up with a few ideas about things. So much could go wrong around here, and really fast at that. No wonder Amelia was so overwhelmed. She'd not only inherited a ranch. She'd inherited a Texas-size mess, too.

Three hours later, they'd found half the cattle, but they didn't find the culprit who'd cut the fence. Thankful they'd acted soon enough to gather most of this small herd of twenty and not the whole big herd on the other side of the ranch. Amelia figured if they'd been a day later, most of Triple R's two hundred head of cattle would have been gathered up and sold at auction or to a slaughterhouse. Cattle rustling was still a thing in Texas and the entire herd had already shrunk since she'd left. She remembered herds running around five hundred head back in the day. Leo must have toned things down to manage better.

She'd need to call the local Special Rangers hired to

work such crimes and alert them that they could have a rustler in their area. They'd recheck with all the sale barns and stations, and they'd keep watch for the distinctive Triple R brand. But she held out little hope of finding her livestock.

Now, she turned to the people who depended on this ranch for jobs, wondering if any of them wanted her out of the way. Especially Ben Nesmith. He'd had a burr in his bonnet and a scowl on his face all day long.

"Listen," she said, motioning for all the men to come forward. "Today, we got robbed. Someone took ten head of cattle, and we know that means thousands of dollars lost. So let's go back over why this happened and also discuss the changes we'll need to make as soon as possible."

Marco stepped forward. "We need to talk to each of you individually." He showed the way to the tack room, which held a small office.

One by one, the men entered and exited after Amelia and Marcus had questioned them.

"I don't know nothing," one said.

"Ben runs a tight ship. He don't like us squealing."

"Would you rather be fired?" Amelia asked.

And so it went. Nothing.

Finally, Tommy, the last one, had told them a few things.

"Ben stays to himself, but lately he's been having a lot of phone calls. Walks off a piece and gets into it with someone. I don't know who, and he's already warned me to stay out of his business. So I might regret telling you that."

"You won't have to regret anything," Amelia had

told the young man. "What you tell us stays between us, understand?"

"Yes, ma'am." Then Tommy shrugged. "It's just that Ben's good to me. Gave me another chance when I'd run out. And Mr. Leo approved and treated me like I was somebody. That man was one of a kind. I don't want to lose this job. I can't."

"You won't," Amelia said. "I won't let that happen, Tommy."

Once they were finished, she asked four men to go in pairs of two to each pasture and call her if they saw anything suspicious. Then she told Ben Nesmith she'd meet with him in the next few days to make a list of needed updates and changes.

He tipped his hand in an exaggerated gesture and spit on the ground before he turned and walked away.

"Thanks, all of you," she told the workers who were still listening. "Go get cleaned up and get something to eat."

Everyone scattered after that. Amelia turned to Marco as they started walking toward the main house. "They aren't happy to see me here."

"They'll get over that. You were amazing. The way you handled Tommy was kind, Amelia. All this on your plate, but you're showing your true colors."

"You mean grumpiness and anti-social tendencies?"

"No, a good heart and the ability to take this ranch to the next level."

"Ben Nesmith doesn't think so."

"I'll handle him for you, ma'am," Marco said in a good cowboy voice.

Amelia gave him a tired smile. "I'm dirty and I'm

sleepy and I'm hungry, so I'm not too worried about Nesmith right now."

Marco glanced at her. "Shower, sleep and food."

"Food, shower, sleep," she said. "I still need to process all of this."

"I'll do some sleuthing," Marco replied. "Start a list of everyone who seems to be gunning for you."

"You haven't had much sleep, either."

"I'm not a good sleeper."

"Thank you for helping today. You're surprisingly good on a horse."

"It's been a while, but hey, it's like riding a bike."

"There's a lot more to you than meets the eye."

"Yeah, a lot more that you don't need to know about."

She raised her eyebrows. "Or maybe I should know about?"

Marco laughed at that, got her back to the house and then told Rosa and Alan what they'd found. "Amelia is on it. We should hear if any Triple R cattle show up on the sale floors or any other place."

He also went over their questioning of the employees. "She handled everything those hands tried to throw at her, too."

"She always was smart," Alan said while Rosa heated up a plate for both of them. "I've called around, too, so I could get some calls regarding the cattle."

"So what did Chastain do after we left?" Marco asked, watching Amelia wash her face and hands at the kitchen sink.

Alan shook his head. "He left, dissatisfied and upset. Said he'd be back first thing tomorrow."

Amelia ran her damp hands over her hair and sat

down to the tamales Rosa had promised earlier. "Samuel likes to get down to business, so yes, we'll meet again tomorrow." After taking a bite of the soft tamales covered in a rich red sauce, she closed her eyes and sighed. "Tomorrow, I'm going to find out everything I can about Leo's sickness and his last days. And then I'm going to search for the people who don't want me here. And the people who took our cattle, too."

She finished her meal, then got up and said, "I'm going to get a shower and then I'm going to sleep."

Marco escorted her to her room. "I hope you really do get some sleep."

"Me, too," she said. "But my head is buzzing with the last twenty-four hours."

"I'll be nearby," he replied. "I talked Rosa into letting me sleep across the hall from you."

Amelia almost protested then shook her head. "I'm too tired to argue with you."

"No argument, no discussion. I need to be near you."

Amelia's expression softened, the tense facade draining away while she stared into his eyes. "Just don't hover too much. I'm a loner. I like to be alone. Well, most of the time anyway."

"And now?" he asked.

"Now, I'm so confused I can't make a coherent decision, but I do appreciate you, Marco."

Then she turned and shut the door in his face.

"Good night," Marco whispered to the door with a smile. She was warming up to him. And he had developed a new appreciation of her, too.

SIX

Amelia woke at three in the morning. She'd heard something outside, or maybe she'd heard something in her scattered dreams. She couldn't be sure what was real and what she'd imagined.

Grabbing an old robe she'd found in the closet, she went to the curtained doors and lifted one of the heavy drapes back out of the way. A man stood at the edge of the courtyard, staring at the house. Staring at her.

With a gasp, she closed the drapery and pulled her robe tightly against her. Blinking, she swallowed the fear clawing at her throat. She could have imagined the man.

Going to a nearby window, she peeked again. The moonlight shined brightly on the plants and bushes surrounding the outdoor furniture. But no one stood in the courtyard this time.

Wide awake now, she carefully opened her bedroom door and hurried toward the kitchen to check out the windows there. If she didn't see anyone, maybe some of Rosa's chamomile tea would help her get back to sleep.

But when she walked in, she gasped. A man sat on

a bar stool at the big counter, a cup of something next to him.

"Marco?"

He whirled and stood. "Yeah?"

"I couldn't sleep," she said, relief washing through her. "Thought I'd make some tea."

He checked her over. "You all right?"

Pushing at her hair, she said, "No, not really. I heard a noise and then when I looked outside, I thought I saw a man standing in the courtyard."

Marco had his back to the windows and doors, but he went to work, grabbing his gun to go out.

"Wait," she said. "He's gone now."

"I'll chase him down."

"He's gone. Don't go out there alone."

"I've done this before."

"I don't want you to go out there, okay?"

He went to the kitchen window and then went to the big glass doors from the dining area. Amelia followed, curious.

The moonlight shifted across the courtyard but neither the moon nor the one bright security light showed anyone there.

"I saw him, and he saw me," she said. "I'm sure he left after that."

"Can you describe him?" Marco asked.

Amelia sank down on a bar stool. "He did look a lot like Daniel. But that can't be. Daniel is dead. I think someone's trying to gaslight me."

Marco turned and came back toward her. "It could be a ranch hand, hired to scare you off. Or someone who knew Leo, trying to get inside the house. But why?"

"No one wants me here, that's for sure. And since

we have about two dozen people on this ranch at any given time, it could take a while to pin someone down."

"We'll beef up security," Marco said. "You can talk to your crew, have them take shifts at the gate and around the house. You should consider an overall security system. The house has good locks on the doors and the windows, but an alarm would be better."

She nodded, then went to make her tea. "This house has never had a security system. Leo never liked them. I'll check into that, too."

He watched while she heated the kettle and picked a tea bag out of the colorful container. "Did you sleep at all?"

She waited for the whistle on the kettle to steam, then brought the hot tea over to the counter. "From nine until now, so four hours maybe. I had strange dreams. I thought I was still dreaming when I glanced outside, but that man was real. Too real. It could have been Daniel standing there."

Marco sat back down beside her. "Tell me about him."

She didn't want to go there, but maybe it would help to talk about things. "Daniel was a good person. Tall, dark blond hair and deep hazel eyes. His father, Kent Parker, wanted him to follow in his footsteps and take over the ranch. They own a smaller ranch a few miles from here."

"So he was your neighbor?"

"Yes, we grew up together—went to the same schools, hung in the same crowds. Things got serious in high school and then college. Park Meadows Ranch is a beautiful place. A big farmhouse and the Chiquita River in the backyard, same as here."

"Daniel was your high school sweetheart?"

She nodded. "Yes, but it went beyond that with us. We loved each other and we made plans for the future. He went on to medical school while I studied photography and worked all kinds of jobs from magazines to newspapers to television stations. I took photos and made a little money while he finished and did his residency at a hospital in Houston. We were going to get married once he'd finished. We took some time and traveled the world, and he helped out with underserved communities everywhere we went. I took photos and filed them with news outlets, hoping to showcase the plight of third world people. We were a team, and we were finally going to have the life we'd talked about."

Marco didn't speak. She glanced over at him, seeing understanding in his eyes. "We came home to get married, and his father wanted him to stay here, to work in a nearby hospital and maybe help out at the ranch as needed. Daniel's mother left a long time ago. She wasn't a very good mother. Daniel never got over that and so he traveled a lot, staying away from the ranch." She shrugged. "We both had our reasons for wanting to leave, as much as we loved our homes."

She took a sip of her tea. "His father didn't approve of me because he knew my parents worked here and that wasn't good enough for Kent Parker. Even though Leo and Siri loved me and treated me as their own, Mr. Parker scorned me. I never understood why. My father was the ranch manager, Leo's right-hand man, and my mother kept up the grounds, did the landscaping. She had her own company. They were both hardworking and successful. We lived in a nice ranch house at the edge of the property. Leo sold that house after my parents died and a nice couple lives there now. Happy."

"Maybe Kent Parker wasn't happy, so he didn't want his son to love someone else more than he loved his daddy."

"That's possible," she said. "He did hover over Daniel, and he sure tried to control him. But Daniel had a bit of his mama's rebel heart, I think."

"So what happened?" Marco said, his voice low. "I mean the night Daniel died?"

She shut her eyes and tried to find her voice, her fingers drifting to the bracelet on her left arm. The pain always hit her like a slap and made her dizzy and nauseated.

"Daniel had a fight with his father and left to come and find me. He told his dad we were adults, and we would get married, with or without Kent's blessings. We planned to elope. After we talked and I'd calmed him down, he left but he had a wreck near the gate to the ranch. His truck went off the road and—technically still on our property—hit a massive oak tree head-on. He wasn't wearing his seat belt."

She stopped, put down her tea. "It was my fault, according to his dad. I'd changed his son, made him want to do crazy things. Made him forget his legacy—the ranch. Kent couldn't blame himself, so he blamed me. I wasn't even allowed to attend Daniel's funeral."

Marco got up and came to her, taking her in his arms. "So you left?"

She nodded and wiped at her eyes. "Leo and I had a fight. He didn't want me to travel anymore, but I couldn't stay here and go past the spot where Daniel died, reliving that night over and over."

"Did you witness the crash?"

She looked up at Marco. "No. I heard the crash, saw

the fire and smoke. Ran down to the road. It was so horrible, fire and twisted metal. There's still a mark in that big oak, a mark left on me, too."

Marco touched her face, wiping away her tears.

She stopped, a mist burning at her eyes. "Daniel, dead. It was unimaginable. Still is. I was so in shock, I thought I saw him walking away from the vehicle. But it was just one of the people who'd come to help." Then she looked up at Marco. "Who would be so cruel, so full of hate, they'd do this to me?"

Marco held her, rubbing a hand down her back. "I'm sorry. So sorry. No wonder you couldn't stay. I don't blame you. And I don't have any answers yet."

"But now I'm back and seeing… Daniel. Rosa saw him, too." She wiped her eyes and looked up at Marco. "We're not imagining this. We've both seen this man. Now I'm wondering what if Daniel didn't die in that wreck? What if the person I saw walking away truly was him?"

Marco knew she wanted to believe that, but his gut told him someone was messing with her. He pulled her over to a couch and sat down with her, hoping to wipe the despair and torment off her pretty face.

"I can dig up the accident report and anything else connected with the accident. It was the only vehicle, correct? Or could someone have forced him off the road?"

"The authorities told us he was alone, no other vehicles involved."

"So what happened? He wouldn't have been speeding, right?"

She shrugged, pushed at her hair. "Daniel was upset when he arrived, but excited when he left. We'd planned to pack up and leave within the week—go someplace tropical and with a beach. I don't know what happened, really. There's a curve about a fourth of a mile from the gate. It can be dangerous if you're speeding. I always wondered if a deer had jumped out and he'd swerved to keep from hitting the animal. But no one ever checked for any hurt or dead animals, and none were found on the road."

Lowering her head, she added, "I rode Buster all through the woods the next day and found nothing. I kept hoping I'd dreamed all of it. But it was real."

"And the authorities just chalked it up to being an accident, without going any further on an investigation?"

"No other investigation, no. The sheriff and the others who showed up said he'd somehow swerved off the road. Claimed his new cell phone must have distracted him. He never answered his phone when he drove. Always cautioned me against doing it."

"So someone could have forced him off the road and left before anyone arrived?"

"Possibly." She lifted her head. "Are you always so suspicious?"

"I have to be. Things are never as they seem."

Amelia curled up on the couch and held her arms across her knees, then studied him for a moment. "I was so upset, so devastated, I never questioned anyone. I just knew Daniel was gone and his father blamed me. I had to leave. Leo and I had an argument because he thought leaving would be the worst thing for me. But… I couldn't stay here. I only came back later for Siri's funeral. I didn't want to come back here ever. And now, after seeing that man in the moonlight, I can't be sure about anything."

"That man is not Daniel," Marco said. "Someone could be wearing a wig or a disguise to make you think that. To make you leave again. To scare you or cause you to look bad—you know—still grieving, too emotional, not in your right mind."

"I get it," she said, lifting off the couch to pace. "And I intend to prove them wrong."

"Now you're talking," he said. "And meantime, I'll do some checking on the accident report and try to piece together what really happened that night."

"Okay, I guess I'll try to get some sleep," she said. "I don't know if that's possible." She glanced back outside, then whirled and grabbed Marco's arm. "Marco, look. Fire!"

Marco grabbed his cell and called 911. "Don't go out there, Amelia," he called as she started toward the fire.

But she was already out the door.

Amelia hurried to where a few extra hay bales were covered and stacked on wooden planks behind one of the outbuildings. It hadn't rained in days and the bales were like kindling, burning hot and exploding in a frenzy of white-hot heat. She heard sirens and saw Rosa and Alan running toward the hay barn. If the whole thing caught on fire, the flames could jump to the stables and beyond. Too much horseflesh to risk losing.

She headed there first, so she could get the horses out into the big fenced pasture behind the stables.

But when she rushed inside, someone grabbed her, his gloved hand covering her mouth. Amelia tried to scream as she twisted away. But he held her tight, dragging her toward the back of the stables. She had to think fast.

Buster's stall was up ahead. The big gelding was already trying to get out, his kicks and high-pitched whinnies showing distress. As the masked man dragged her close, she lifted her body toward the stall, grabbing onto the door to try and open it. The man tugged at her, but she held to the stall's sliding door until she'd managed to pull it back.

"Stop it," the man hissed in her ear. "You should have stayed away."

Nesmith? It didn't sound like him. He tugged at her, trying to lift her. Amelia held to the door, splinters cutting her hands until she had it open enough for Buster to escape.

Her ribs ached as the man put pressure on her stomach so he could pry her away. Amelia lifted a leg and managed to twist it around his, tripping him. With a grunt the man fell away, Amelia toppling over with him. She grabbed at the dirt floor and crawled to the side as Buster shot out of the stall and kicked over the man, causing him to cry out in pain.

Amelia tried to breathe, her whole body on fire and her hands bleeding from the rough doors she'd held on to.

Then she heard footsteps running through the alley, and sirens echoing off in the distance.

"Amelia?"

"Marco," she tried to call. "Over here."

The man stood, wobbling, then pulled a gun out and aimed it toward Amelia. She screamed. Marco shot.

The man fell to the ground.

The next thing she knew, Marco had her in his arms

as he ran with her away from the stables. She saw the fire leaping toward the building.

"Horses," she said.

"The others are getting them out and the fire department just arrived."

Marco held her tight and didn't stop until they were well away from the burning hay barn.

"The stables?"

"Safe for now."

Finally he found a bench and lowered her down. "What were you thinking?"

"That I had to save my livestock," she said, tears streaming down her face.

"You can't be this reckless, Amelia. You could have been killed."

"I fought him off," she said, then she winced.

Marco lifted her hands, saw the blood and scratches. "Where else do you hurt?"

She looked down at the dirt gouged into her bracelet. That made her angry. She checked each charm—the Lone Star, the tiny Triple R ranch brand, the bluebonnets symbols, the one holding the initials "DP loves AG" with an oak tree etched into the silver.

"All over," she admitted. "I fought."

"I saw you fighting," he replied, his fingers wiping away dirt and tears. He lifted his T-shirt and cleaned the pretty charms. "At least your bracelet survived." He studied it, knowing it must be special to her.

Amelia let him clean her up. "And you shot him?"

"Yeah, I did."

"Is he dead?"

"I hope so."

She grabbed onto Marco and held tight. "You've saved me again."

Marco sat back on the bench and held her close, so close she could feel the rapid beats of his heart. "I reckon I did at that."

Rosa came running, her Spanish rapid, but Amelia didn't need to know what she was saying. Marco explained what had happened and Rosa insisted they get her inside.

"I'll handle the authorities for now." Marco lifted Amelia up and carried her to the house.

While the hay barn went up in smoke behind them.

SEVEN

"The good news is the man I shot in the stables is alive and talking," Marco told Amelia the next morning. "The bad news is that he's refusing to tell us who hired him."

"Did he start the fire?"

Amelia had barely slept, but the fire department had saved the stables and main barn, at least. The sheriff had promised a report this morning, and Marco and Alan had just talked to one of the sheriff deputies. Amelia planned to get a full report after she checked out the scene later in the light of day.

"He won't admit to it, but the fire chief seems to think so, yes." He shrugged. "And I'm wondering if he could be the one who drove all the way to East Texas to shoot at you and set the cabin on fire, too."

Amelia held her coffee mug close. Her hands, still raw and torn from her efforts to get away from that man last night, had bandages on them. Rosa had insisted after she spotted Amelia's injuries last night. But Amelia hadn't agreed to be bandaged until this morning when everything she touched brought searing pain. Now she felt like she was wearing fingerless gloves.

"Well, that figures. He's scared, too, then. Good. Let him worry and lose sleep along with the rest of us."

"I'd rather he talks and saves himself and us." Marco came and sat down at the table with her, where the view to the courtyard looked pristine and bright in the light of day. "So he wasn't the same man you saw out the window last night?"

"No." She'd caught a glimpse of the medics carrying her attacker away from the stables on a stretcher. "Heavier, and with less hair. But his voice sounded almost like Ben Nesmith's."

"Speaking of Ben, he's a no-show today."

"Seriously?" She had to wonder if Ben could be responsible for her misery. "If he's behind this, what could he possibly gain?"

"A lot, if someone's paying him to sabotage the ranch and harm you."

"And you're sure he's not here today?"

"Yes," Marco responded. "Didn't report in this morning, but Alan told the workers to go about their work while he calls the insurance adjuster about the fire. The fire chef can't find the origin, but he believes it had to have been set. Good thing y'all stored hay in several locations."

"For this very reason," she said, thinking about yet another busy day searching for answers. "If we store it too tight and without air, it molds quickly, but too dry, it becomes a fire risk. So we store some inside out of the weather and a few bales here and there around the property as needed, the bottom layers loosened and scattered so it can dry out. That helped fuel the fire last night, however."

"Yep." He sipped his coffee and stared at her. "I'm

gonna see if I can locate your missing foreman. I suggest you take it easy today. Samuel is coming back to read the will this afternoon, and we don't need any more interruptions."

"No, we don't. But this was just our first day and night. No telling what we have in store for us today."

"You have a strange sense of humor."

"I'm being realistic. But I'm not going to sit around waiting. I can't focus on the ranch with someone out to get me."

"Hopefully, they'll back off since the locals and I are all over it."

She watched him, liking the easy way he dealt with life. "Tell me more about your family, Marco."

He checked his watch. "Will you look at the time."

"No, don't do that, don't brush me off. You know all about me, but I only know a little about you."

His dark eyebrows winged up. "Am I a suspect, Amelia?"

She mimicked him by raising her eyebrows. "Not yet."

He got up and poured them both some more coffee. "Well, you know the farm was near San Antonio. I can't call it a ranch, but we had some acreage and a few crops, couple of cows, chickens, the works."

"And horses?"

"Nope. We had a neighbor who raised horses. I worked for him after school a lot to make money. That's where I learned to ride and act out my cowboy daydreams."

Amelia could only imagine Marco as a young man. Now she'd have cowboy daydreams, too. About the man he'd turned out to be. To tamp down her awareness, she said, "You're industrious, aren't you?"

"I had to be back then," he replied, his dark eyes bittersweet. "I guess I still am. Like I told you, Daddy wasn't much of a farmer, and really, he wasn't much of a dad and husband, either. Went from halfway farming to odd jobs here and there. Things weren't good. A lot of fights and a whole lot of anger. He died and left us nothing. So I've been working hard for years now to keep that land. My mama wanted to move because it was so isolated, so she's in a safe place now. I had the house torn down, but I can't bring myself to sell the land. Her land now."

"That's noble. You're a good son."

"I wasn't always a good man, Amelia. But when I came home after my years in the Army, the police officer who helped me took me under his wing as an informant. He also got me going to church with his family. That led to me becoming a private investigator. I work mostly with the sheriff's department around Dallas and Fort Worth and then back in Austin and San Antonio. And I take on cases from private clients, such as you. Although I've never been involved in anything like this."

"We set the bar high around here," she retorted. "I trust you, Marco. You've obviously had lots of experience in your line of work. But if you're going to look for Ben Nesmith, I'm going with you."

"I don't think—"

"—I'm going. He works for the ranch and if he's involved in this, he's going to have to admit it to my face."

"I don't think he'll admit to anything."

"He will if I threaten to fire him."

Marco stared her down. "You're the boss. I have his address and I'm leaving in ten minutes."

She stood and took her dishes to the sink. "I'll be ready in five."

Rosa came through and stopped. "You need rest, Amelia. Let the others handle this." She lifted one of Amelia's hands. "We need to freshen your bandages."

"I can't rest," Amelia replied, gently pulling her hand away. "Not until I know what's going on and find a way to stop it."

"Obstinado." Rosa shook her head, her silky salt-and-pepper messy bun bouncing. "I expect you to rest at least a little. You have bruised ribs. And later, we can have a nice dinner. Samuel will be joining us."

"I'll be fine," Amelia said. "You know I can't sit still."

Rosa smiled. *"Si,* always in motion, this one."

Marco frowned. "I'm beginning to understand that, yeah."

Ben Nesmith lived in a small house on the edge of Colón property. Marco had directions from one of the workers.

"It's the foreman's house. Near where the river narrows to the west."

Apparently, that and the mailbox numbers would get Marco to the house. Amelia knew the way, too. She sort of sank against her seat. "My parents' old house is about mile farther out. But I haven't been there in a long time. Daniel and I—" she stopped, took a breath "—used to fish and swim there."

Marco let her have a moment to remember, thinking these memories were going to keep popping up, and maybe that could help her to heal. He hoped so.

He knew about memories bubbling to the surface like oil creeping through water. They could destroy you or force you to run away from yourself. She'd run, and fast. Now she had to slow down and relive everything all over.

Same way he relived fighting for his country and all the baggage that came with that—baggage mixed with pride made life messy at times.

Lord, I haven't asked for much lately, but we sure could use some help here.

Asking for a prayer to be answered felt odd, rusty, and distant. But he took a deep breath and kept asking.

Amelia glanced at him. "You okay over there?"

He nodded. "Yep. Just running through a few thoughts. Do you ever pray about things?"

"Whoa, where did that come from?"

"I know I don't look like the praying kind," he said, "but we need some intervention here."

She smiled. "Yes, we do. And yes, I pray. Siri and Leo took me to church and Rosa backed that up with her own sage wisdom and a few references to the Word when I needed to hear that."

"Okay, so we're on the same page here, even if I'm the biggest backslider on the Lord's list."

"I might be somewhere behind you, but I'm never far from my faith. Sometimes, it's the only thing I have left. Like now, with my cabin back east burned and a barnful of valuable hay gone. I'm gonna need all the faith I can muster."

He gave her a quick smile.

She pointed to the road. "The foreman's house is just up ahead on the right."

Marco pulled his truck into the long gravelly driveway. A medium-size short-haired dog ran barking along with the vehicle.

"He still has that dog," Amelia said. "Puff, I believe is his name."

"His teeth show more than puff," Marco replied.

"He's harmless, or he was when he was younger."

They got out and he noticed Amelia wincing. "You should have stayed home."

"Stop babying me. I'm okay. I need to keep at it, or I'll fall apart."

"Just stop being so reckless."

"Look," she said, "you don't have to do this. I can handle this on my own. I have to, Marco. For Leo's sake, at least. He trusted me enough to leave the ranch to me, so I have to fight for it. And I've learned I can't always depend on anyone else. It's up to me."

"That's what I'm afraid of," Marco said. "You out there all alone, fighting for a ranch you didn't even want. It's dangerous. Or maybe you want it to be dangerous, as punishment or something? Because you left. And because you're still standing. The last one."

She glared at him, her eyes dancing fire. "Stop analyzing me and let's see if Ben's at home."

She hurried toward the dog, rubbing his tan coat. "What's wrong, Puff? Did Ben forget to feed you?"

Marco reluctantly followed. The woman never listened to anyone, but he'd make sure he was with her as much as possible. Maybe this had become a quest, a reason to fight with her. He'd gotten caught in the middle of something more than a man leaving an inheritance to a woman he loved like a daughter. There were so many variables here, Marco couldn't walk away.

That…and he couldn't walk away from Amelia just yet, either, no matter all the warning signs and reminders that he didn't do this. He didn't go all in on falling for someone he'd only known about twenty-four long hours.

They made it the door, Puff on their trail. The dog barked more frantically now, his paws scratching at the door.

Amelia gave Marco a concerned frown. "Something's wrong."

She gingerly tried the handle and the door swung open. Puff rushed past her, still barking.

The door creaked all the way in, then banged against the wall. The house was still and warm, too still, too warm.

Marco pulled out his gun and tried to tug her back. He moved to step past her. "Wait, okay?"

But she didn't stop. She marched right in. "Nesmith, I need to talk to you."

Amelia stopped so quickly, he shoved into her, her bandaged hands going to her face. "Marco?"

Marco followed her gaze to the place near an old battered coffee table where Puff had stopped and now sat whining.

Ben Nesmith lay face down on the living room floor in a pool of blood, a gunshot wound to his back. He wouldn't be telling them anything today, after all. Ben was dead and from the looks of it, he'd been dead for a while now.

But then Marco realized what had really upset Amelia so much. The letter *D* written in blood by Ben's body.

EIGHT

Amelia's hands shook as she tried to take the bottle of water from one of the deputies who'd arrived on the scene. Marco had called it in right away, and while they waited he'd gone over the house looking for clues or possible evidence.

"I think Ben knew his assailant," he whispered to her while the deputies and crime scene people did their job. They'd both been questioned since they'd found the body. "The door was open, the dog was out, nothing is stolen. Not even any show of a struggle or a fight." He eyed the spot where they'd found the foreman. "And shot in the back, at that."

Amelia glanced at the floor across the room. The medical examiner had already taken the body away, but she could see the line the crime techs had drawn, an outline of Ben's body. That and the blood—how could she ever end this nightmare?

"Yes, someone whose name starts with the letter *D*." Her heart shook each time she thought about seeing Daniel out the window. "It can't be. I know Daniel's gone. Someone here is messing with us. Ben must have known the truth."

"I don't believe Daniel is here, Amelia. If he were alive, he'd come to you and let you know. You two loved each other, so why would he torment you?" Marco glanced around and then said, "The accident report I got doesn't show much more than what you've already told me. The only thing that stood out—the truck shouldn't have caught fire so quickly."

"What? It hit a tree and exploded on impact. That's what we were told."

"It exploded, but he wasn't going that fast. I think he swerved to avoid hitting a person, and that person could have…finished him off."

"How? With a match and leaking gasoline?"

"It's a possibility."

She shook her head. "I can see what you're saying. But what if Daniel got out of the truck before this person set fire to it? What if he'd been hiding out and now he knows I'm back?"

"He'd let you know in a way that didn't involve stalking, shooting and more fires to put out, don't you think?"

"I don't know," she admitted. "Logic tells me it's not him, but I'm tired, confused and still in shock. Maybe I'm imagining things."

"I think you're spot-on, not imagining. Someone is gaslighting you big-time. And I think Ben could have been in on it, or he found out and they didn't want him to talk." Marco looked around the house and back to her. "They got in, shot him and got out."

"So someone who knew him, someone he trusted, did this?"

"It looks that way to me," Marco said. "But the deputies are sweeping the whole house and the outbuildings for anything, any DNA, fibers, blood, a weapon—you know it, they're looking for it. They won't tell us anything, of course."

"But what if they don't find anything? How am I ever supposed to get on with my life? I'm still trying to wrap my brain around Leo's death and now I'm supposed to take over the ranch. Now that I've been back, I can see it's declining. Leo had to have been really sick to let the ranch go into disrepair."

"Yeah, about that," Marco said. "My gut isn't liking that Leo died from natural causes."

"Stop," she said, slamming her water bottle down so hard one of the first responders glanced over at her. "You're used to conspiracy theories in your line of work, right? Stop trying to come up with even more problems than I already have."

"Can't you see it?" he asked. "First Daniel, then Leo, Siri and now the foreman. Too many people are dying around here, Amelia. How can you think you're seeing Daniel and not realize something doesn't add up?"

"Daniel died of a horrible accident," she said, wondering why he was so obsessed with this thread. "And Siri had cancer. I haven't had time to dig into what caused Leo's death. But I can't do this and make it through what lies ahead. So stop."

"Just think about that night when Daniel died. You might remember something, anything that could help."

"I remember all of it," she said. Then she got up and moved away from him.

"Why are you two arguing?" one of the deputies asked. "Do you know more about this than you're letting on?"

Marco heaved a sigh. "Miss Garcia has been shot at, had her cabin back in East Texas burned to the ground and a barn on her property here burned last night, she was attacked near that barn, and now her ranch foreman is dead. We came here to talk to him about who might have set fire to the ranch's hay barn last night." Glancing at Amelia, he added, "I asked one too many questions about this whole affair and, understandably, she's tired and upset and doesn't have the answers. My bad."

Amelia heard the whole conversation, amazed that he'd take the blame to protect her even after she'd gotten angry.

She whirled to come back, her eyes on the young deputy. "Strange things have been happening at the Rio Rojo Ranch. Now, this. Ben was a good man. He'd worked on the ranch for years. He resented me taking over, but he was willing to do the work."

"He resented you?" the deputy said. The deputy's gaze took in her bandaged hands. "Did you two have words?"

"Enough," Marco said. "She's in danger. She was injured yesterday trying to save her animals. Whoever did this really wants her dead, too." He filled the deputy in on everything. "Look, we talked to the authorities last night after the fire. Right now, we need to get back to the ranch."

The deputy finally nodded. "Stay close. We might need to go over this again."

"We found Ben, but we didn't kill him," Amelia said. "Trace our hands for gunpowder residue. You won't find any."

Marco shot her a warning glance. The deputy had his eyes on her, not Marco, thankfully. "I'm sorry, ma'am, for giving you that indication. Your PI here showed us his weapon. It hasn't been fired recently from the looks of it. And you obviously didn't bring a weapon, right?"

"Of course I didn't bring a weapon," she retorted. "There is no GPR on my hands or clothes. Puff—the dog—led us to Ben's body."

The deputy finally gave up, but Amelia figured the authorities wouldn't be finished with her yet.

"This person," she told Marco once they'd been cleared to leave the scene, "could possibly try to make it look like one of us killed Ben. I hope I didn't just dig myself into that hole."

Marco gave her a quick glance. "I think you scared that rookie enough that he wouldn't dare question you again. But the sheriff might. Just be prepared."

"At this point, I won't be surprised about anything," she said. "We need to meet with Samuel and get the details of the will. I have a lot of decisions to make."

"Let's get back to the ranch," Marco said. "You can rest, and I'll take care of the details on Ben's death."

"I can't believe he's dead, and I can't believe that deputy implied we could be responsible."

"Everyone's a suspect right now," Marco replied, his words full of fire.

She'd been running from a killer, but now she had to wonder if coming back to the ranch had put her exactly where the killer wanted her to be. Had she just fallen into a trap?

Marco came out from his room to find Samuel in the kitchen talking with Rosa and Alan. "You're early," he said, checking his watch before he shook hands with Samuel.

The distinguished-looking lawyer's handshake was firm. "I heard about the barn fire and about Ben's death. I got here as soon as I could. I'm glad you're all okay. And glad you decided to stick around, Marco."

"Yeah, me, too." Marco glanced around for Amelia.

Rosa caught his eye. "I made her go and rest. She's still bruised from last night. She should be here soon."

He had seen her shut her door when he'd come up the hallway. She'd insisted on bringing Puff back to the main house and had fixed the poor dog a bed in her room and set up a complete pet kitchen in her bathroom. Puff was getting the royal treatment.

Marco thought her mothering the dog was her way of coping. Underneath that tough veneer, she had a big heart. A broken heart. He wished he could fix that.

Samuel gave him a once-over. "Let's go into the office and get this part out of the way when she does get here. I'd like to enjoy this wonderful dinner Rosa has cooked up while Amelia and I can talk in peace. She must have so many questions, and with this danger hanging over her head, too. Ben was loyal to this ranch, so I'm sure the workers will take this hard."

Marco hoped they'd all have a quiet dinner, but each night brought some sort of threat. The ranch workers had volunteered to watch the place, but any one of them could be involved in this vendetta. They were hard workers and loyal, but they weren't used to the Old West style of walking and riding a ranch with rifles at the ready.

Studying Samuel, he said, "I have some questions, too. But we'll save that for later." He wanted to know how involved Samuel was in the day-to-day operations on the ranch. The lawyer seemed to stay busy, but he might have more than one reason to get Amelia home. But Marco would keep that to himself since Amelia wasn't ready to hear any more conspiracy theories.

He heard Puff running up the hallway and turned to find Amelia walking toward him wearing a flowery flowing dress and battered cowgirl boots, her hair caught up in a twisted bun that made her look even prettier. But her bandages were gone, allowing him to see the dark scratches on her palms and fingers.

"Did you manage to get some rest?" he asked by way of a greeting.

She nodded. "I dozed, had bad dreams, got up and got dressed. I'm here."

Samuel hugged her and then looked at her hands. "Mercy, Amelia, I heard about the fire, but you look like you wrestled with a bear."

"Just a man who's not talking," she said. "Unless someone has made him talk since the last we heard."

Marco shook his head. "Gregory Tyson is still in the hospital under lock and key, and he refuses to talk. Has a long list of petty crimes to his name. Claims he was just trying to steal things to pawn off. But we know that's not the truth."

Rosa motioned to them. "Go take care of business and then we'll enjoy this roast and the cake I made for dessert."

Samuel nodded. "Can you put the food on warm, Rosa? You and Alan need to hear this, too."

Surprised, Marco wondered why Samuel hadn't mentioned this the first time he'd come by. But they had been interrupted. He hoped that wouldn't be the case tonight.

Amelia fell in place beside him as they headed down the hallway toward the big office. He could tell she didn't like this part of the house. Leo's office was next to the primary bedroom where he'd slept and died, and Siri's studio was across the way with a view of the hills and vistas beyond. Amelia gave him a glance mixed with dread and expectation. She did have a big weight on her shoulders. This place didn't come easy. It involved a lot of hard work. She'd need help from all directions.

He'd miss this place and her once this was over.

But then, that was the plan, and it would remain the plan.

He'd have no reason to stay here once she was safe.

He wished for a reason, and when Amelia glanced at him again, this time with more intensity, he thought he knew what that one reason could be. If she asked him to stay, he just might say yes.

Amelia listened with a nervous energy while Samuel read the formal part of the will. She'd avoided this because hearing Leo's last will and testament meant he was really gone. Just like her parents, Daniel and Siri. And now Ben.

Maybe Marco was on to something with all these deaths, but her logical mind couldn't conceive why anyone would be so cruel.

Samuel cleared his throat, his eyes on Rosa and Alan. "Leo especially wanted you both to know this will always be your home. If you don't want to continue on in the main house, he had deeded five acres of land for you to build a home—the funding will come from his estate whenever you're ready. And he also set up modest trust funds for your two sons and their children." He named the amount of each trust fund.

Rosa started crying, while Alan looked shocked as he gripped his wife's hand. "That's Leo. Always so generous. I sure miss him."

"He loved both of you and he loved watching your sons grow up and prosper," Samuel continued. "You can think about this and decide what you want to do later," Samuel said. "The land is yours, so you could build a nice getaway right by the river. I know your grandchildren would love that."

Rosa nodded and sniffed. "*Sí*, they would."

Then Samuel glanced at Amelia. "The rest is pretty straightforward. All of the current workers get a bonus and you, my dear, have inherited the entire ranch and this house, including Siri's artwork. Leo thinks it will be in good hands and that you will honor the legacy of the Rio Rojo."

"Meaning I won't ever be able to sell?"

"Are you considering that?" Samuel asked, surprise in his tone.

"I haven't yet, but this ranch needs a lot of work. I'm not sure where to begin, but I've made some notes."

Samuel nodded. "Well, you have the bank account, too, and it's substantial." He named the total amount of assets.

Amelia couldn't speak. She'd just become a multimillionaire. "I don't know what to say."

"You don't need to say anything," Samuel replied.

"It's all yours, whether you keep it or not. But you might consider since someone is doing their dead-level best to sabotage and possibly harm you, they must be after this ranch and Leo's assets for themselves."

"One intruder shot and in the hospital, one ranch worker dead and a barn fire," Marco said. "Not to mention the lurkers in the courtyard and the person or persons who shot at us at your cabin and then burned it down when they didn't kill us."

Amelia gave him a warning glance. She did not want him to mention his suspicions to anyone else. Because like him, right now she couldn't trust anyone on this ranch.

He took the hint. "But we're working on getting that problem under control, one way or another."

Samuel lifted his chin in agreement. "Let me know if I can help in any way."

Marcus leaned in. "You might be able to tell me if you know of anyone who'd stand between Amelia and this ranch. Who out there thinks this place should be theirs?"

Amelia glanced from Samuel to Rosa and Alan. They'd all glanced back and forth during Marco's question.

"Do any of you know something you're not telling us?" she asked.

Rosa turned to Alan. He said, "We're concerned about these episodes where both you and Rosa have seen a man who looks like Daniel."

"I'm concerned about that, too," she said. "Alan, do you know who he is?"

Alan shot Samuel a stare. "I don't."

"Samuel, do you?"

Samuel turned to Amelia. "I don't, honey. I agree someone's messing with you, but I can't prove it and I do not have any idea about who could be pretending. But we are all concerned regarding Kent Parker."

"Kent Parker?" Marco said, his frown widening. "Daniel's dad? Do you have reason to believe he could be involved?"

Amelia felt sick. "Could he be behind all of this?"

Rosa took Amelia's hand. "After Daniel's funeral, Leo refused to speak to Kent again. Leo was angry that Kent blamed you and kept you from the funeral. He knew Daniel's death wasn't your fault, but he seemed to know more than he wanted to say about what really happened that night."

Amelia stood and started pacing before the empty fireplace. "That makes no sense. Leo was angry with Kent, and he told me he never wanted to speak to Kent again because of how he'd treated me, but I figured they'd let it go by now. Besides, why would Kent come after me now?"

"Because he's still bitter and grieving and he wouldn't like you returning to take over the ranch," Samuel said. "But I'm trying to figure out what he thinks he could gain here. If you're out of the way, does he plan to swoop in on the ranch? He has no say there. He could try to buy it outright or at auction if it came to that, but I doubt he has the capital to pull that off."

"Or he could just want me dead. Period. End of discussion," Amelia said. "The ranch might survive, and he'd have his revenge. He hated me the first time Daniel took me to meet him, and he won't ever get over Daniel's death. But then, neither will I."

She turned and ran out of the room, her heart too heavy to think someone would come up with such a vendetta.

And all because she and Daniel had been in love.

NINE

"I'll go check on her," Marco said, turning to hurry after Amelia. She'd only had a few days to deal with this, and sooner or later, she'd crash and burn.

He found her in the courtyard, watching the sunset touching the hills and trees with painted rays of orange and pink. "Hey, you okay?"

She shook her head. "No. I never wanted this. But if Kent Parker's heard the news of Leo's death and my inheritance, he'd want me gone and fast. The man never liked me. He expected his son to marry up, you know."

"I'd think marrying you would be way up there," Marco said.

She pivoted to give him an unabashed stare. "Have you ever been in love?"

"Not yet, but close. Only she walked away because, well, I have commitment issues and I stay out on jobs too much—to sum up her words. So as I said, not yet." Then he took a breath. "But so close."

Their eyes locked. The wind picked up and caused the chimes and the gurgling fountain water to create a merging melody.

Marco tugged her close. "Amelia…"

"Not yet," she said, her finger touching his lips. "I have to have everything in its proper place, Marco. That's how I operate. This…and you…have thrown my need to keep things tidy and easy into a pile of mush."

"I can see where running from a murderer could turn you to mush, but me? I don't usually have that effect on people."

"You are a strong presence," she admitted. "You're growing on me."

"I've never had a woman tell me that before. Like a barnacle or like an annoying vine?"

"Like a person I want to spend time with when my head is on straight again. This news happened too fast, and now my feelings regarding you are spinning inside my head. I need time."

Marco let that request soak in, regret and relief warring in his head. "You're right. We both need to think this through. It could be the adrenaline, the tension that started the night we met—not the best way to figure out a relationship. Or start one."

"I'm glad you agree," she replied, disappointment in her gaze. Then she changed as fast as the Texas wind. "Do you think Daniel is alive?"

"No," he said. "I think someone wants you to believe that."

"But what if he is alive?" She shrugged. "We were good together and somebody knows that. But what if it's him out there, trying to get a message to me. What if he needs my help?"

Marco understood now, hearing the plea of hope in her words. "You're pushing me away because if by chance Daniel is back, you could pick up where you left off."

Her silence shouted volumes. She looked away, out

toward the setting sun. "I don't know what I want any-more."

"Hey?"

She touched a hand to his arm to stop him from speaking any further. "I told you, I like things tidy and easy, and nothing about any of this is easy. I have to know, Marco. I have to find out what's happening here, and I have a feeling it will hurt me, good or bad. I don't want to drag you into something we'd both regret."

Marco took the gut punch. Then he said, "I'll find out the truth, Amelia. I always do. You need to under-stand that about me. I don't stop until I have every-thing out there—the raw, honest truth. And I'll start with Kent Parker."

"No," she said. "You stay away from him. He could be dangerous."

"Just like you to warn me, when you'll probably go after him as soon as you can."

"We could go together," she said. "Just ask a few questions. His ranch is the closest one, and he might have seen something, heard something."

"Now you're speaking my language," he replied. "Let's go eat so Rosa won't be so sad."

"You just want some of her roast, right?"

"Yep. You can see right through me."

"You'd be smart to remember that."

He took her hands one at a time, checking on her injuries. Then he kissed a few of her cuts, loving her gasp of surprise and the hard-to-read glow in her eyes as led her back inside the house.

Rosa hugged her when she came into the kitchen. "I'm sorry if we upset you before."

"It's not that," Amelia said. "It's the thought that our

neighbor could be the one trying to scare me away. I don't scare easily, but I need to hear anything to help us find these culprits. We can add Kent Parker to the suspect list."

Marco glanced around. "Where's Alan?"

"He got a call to the stables. One of the horses is acting up. He'll be back soon."

Samuel came out of the office. "Okay, business is done and I'm starving. I could smell that roast when I turned into the lane. Rosa's smoked roast is like brisket mixed with filet mignon and has a one-of-a-kind taste."

Rosa smile at Samuel. "It's a Rio Rojo tradition."

They gathered around the table to wait for Alan when Rosa's phone rang.

She gasped and turned to Samuel and Marco. "It's Alan. Someone hit him over the head when he went to check the stables. We need to go. He didn't sound good."

"You two stay here," Marco said. "In case someone is messing with us again."

Rosa nodded and went to a closet to pull out a shotgun. "We'll be here. Hurry, pronto."

"I'm okay," Alan said after Marco and Samuel found him sitting in a corner, holding his head in his hands. "They ran out after I fought back."

"Where is all the help?" Marcus asked, glancing around. "I thought we had guards everywhere."

"Just at the main entries and in all the pastures," Samuel said. "Alan told me that earlier. Most of the hands are in their apartments in the bunkhouse."

Marco glanced toward the horseshoe shape of the apartments across from the barns. "Maybe someone saw something."

"The river," Alan said. "The man's shoes were wet. He must have come by boat."

Marco's heart lurched. "Then this could have been a distraction so someone could get in the house. Samuel, take care of Alan and ask the hands if they saw anything."

"I'm on it," Samuel said, checking Alan's head.

Marco took off toward the main house in a run.

He should have seen this one coming. He'd suggested Amelia and Rosa stay in the house. Now they were alone and possibly about to be ambushed.

He rushed through the back door and into the kitchen, stopping short when he saw Rosa holding her gun on a scrawny young man, Amelia right behind her with a heavy frying pan.

"They're gonna kill me," the man said. "I don't want no part of this."

"Part of what?" Amelia asked. "He was about to tell us."

Marco pulled out his gun. "You'd better start talking or I'll shoot."

The man swallowed. "They offered me a hundred dollars to sneak in and leave that letter on the counter."

Marco checked the counter by the other door where a white envelope lay. "I see. Who were they?"

"I don't know. A man with sunglasses and dark blond hair. But he had on a hat. He gave me the envelope and told me my money would be waiting in a bag next to the courtyard gate."

"Did you find the money?"

The man nodded. "Yeah, and I'm keeping it."

"We'll let the sheriff consider that," Marco said, reaching for his phone. "Everyone here is tired of being stalked and threatened, understand? So if you're holding out on me, it won't be good."

"I just needed some spending money," the man told them, his dark eyes full of fear and dread. "The man found me walking along the road. He was in an old pickup. He told me it'd be easy."

"Do these two women look easy?"

"No, sir."

"Do yourself a favor, kid. Tell the officers the truth and give them a good description of the person who hired you."

Samuel and Alan came in, Alan holding a cloth to his head. Rosa put down her gun and ran to her husband.

"One of the workers saw someone leaving the barn but didn't recognize him. Thought he could be a vendor. Didn't bother to check," Samuel said. Then he glanced at the teenager with Marco. "Who is this?"

"An interloper," Marco replied. "But Rosa and Amelia had things under control."

He held the boy, waiting for someone to come and take him in for questioning.

"It's been chaotic since Ben's gone," Alan said while his wife fussed with the cut on his forehead. "People quitting or coming and going. I've had a hard time keeping up. Someone lured me there and then tried to bash my head in."

"You can say that again," Marco replied, tugging the boy forward. "Let's get this one to the sheriff. Maybe then, we can finally sit down and have a meal without someone trying to harm us."

"I can't go back to jail," the man shouted as Marco

led him toward the sirens in the front yard. "I can't. I just needed some easy money."

"Money, just like women, is never easy," Marco said. "You need to learn that lesson."

He glanced back to see Amelia staring at the envelope on the counter.

"Well, if we can get the man in the hospital to talk, we might be able to form a case against your tormentors," he told Amelia later at dinner. No one seemed hungry now, but they made the effort to eat. "All these tricks and upsets are just a smoke screen, Amelia."

Amelia glanced at the envelope again. She and Rosa had put on rubber gloves to open it. A picture of her and Daniel together, laughing, happy, in love.

Marco's stomach roiled with that knowledge—she still loved Daniel Parker, and someone was pushing that love to the limit in a cruel way.

"Scare tactics," she replied, her finger tearing at the crusty bread Rosa had baked earlier. "I'm not going anywhere. In fact, the more they come after me, the harder I'll dig in my heels."

Yet she still stared at that envelope as if it were a spider crawling toward her.

"I was afraid of that," Samuel said. "I wish I could address your questions and concerns. I'm as shocked as you are about this. What I can do is have a talk with Kent Parker."

Amelia glanced at Marco. "That might be a good idea. But don't mention our suspicions. Just let him know I now own the ranch, but I don't want any trouble. Maybe ask him if he's heard or seen anyone suspicious lurking around. I plan to stay away from him, and he can do the same with me."

Marco felt relief that she seemed to change her mind about confronting Kent herself. That would set off all kinds of alarms and even more problems.

"I'll handle it," Samuel said. "You can count on me."

Marco wondered about the gentleman lawyer. Could he be in on this, too, so he could somehow cash in on getting the ranch away from Amelia? Hard to believe, but anything was feasible at this point.

TEN

Later that night, after Samuel and Marco had brought in some deputies to moonlight as paid patrols near the front gate, Amelia got up and went to the big doors leading from her room to the big courtyard. Glancing down at the picture of her and Daniel from a few years ago, she decided she needed some air. She opened the door and stepped out into the warm night. The sky was full of twinkling stars and the wind whispered in her ear like a hand touching her.

She stood close to the open door, but when she heard a noise on the other side of the yard, her heart lifted. Would Daniel show up tonight? Would he approach her? But then, her heart hit bottom. Would he try to hurt her or worse?

She turned toward the noise and saw a man coming toward her. Taking in a breath, Amelia braced herself to find Daniel alive. Or to confront her tormentor.

"Amelia?"

Marco stepped out of the shadow, wearing a black T-shirt and old jeans.

"You scared me," she said, disappointment mixing with anticipation in her heart.

"You shouldn't be out here," he replied, moving close.

"I needed some air. Did I make too much noise?"

"No. I heard a door creaking open. Guess it was yours."

"So neither of us should be out here."

"Probably not. I guess we both had the same idea." Then he glanced toward the back gate. "Or were you hoping to see someone else?"

"Honestly, I don't know," she said. "I've stared at that old photo for an hour or so. I can't sleep. I'm so torn about everything." Then because her heart was hurting and she needed something, someone, to lean on, she whispered, "Especially you."

Marco pulled her into his arms. "Let me set you straight on that one." He kissed her, his hands pulling through her hair, his lips touching on hers with a deep intensity that left her warm and secure and longing for more.

Amelia sighed into the kiss, letting her heart guide her.

She fit into his arms in a way that made her feel safe and sure.

But could he fit into her world?

She pulled away to stare up at him. "We were supposed to wait on this."

"I'm an impatient man."

"I can certainly see that."

He touched his finger to her cheek. "I thought that would clear my head, but it backfired on me."

"How so?"

"I'm still mixed up."

"So am I," she replied. Then because she wanted him to understand, she glanced around the courtyard.

"I know that Daniel is dead, but my heart still wonders about all the things that brought me back here."

"I brought you back here," he said with a chuckle. "I never imagined any of this, however."

"You should get a big bonus."

He tugged her back into his arms. "Oh, I already have that."

They kissed again, and while Amelia loved his kisses, his kindness, his protection, she knew she'd need to turn to her faith to get her through this— weighing the past and the future—and what that could mean for her now.

The cell phone in her pocket started buzzing. Pulling away from Marco, she stared down at the unknown number.

"Let it go to voice mail," he said. "'Cause nothing good can be on the other side of that phone after midnight."

She hesitated and then decided he was right. "Maybe it's a wrong number."

When she saw the voice mail pop up, she glanced at Marco. "Will you listen with me?"

"If you don't mind."

She hit the button and held her breath while she listened.

"That was a big mistake, Amelia. How can you kiss another man when I'm here waiting?"

Amelia dropped her phone. It hit the rug under their feet with a clatter. Marco tugged her close and held her there.

"Daniel's voice?" he asked.

She nodded. "So familiar, but…so sinister now."

Marco picked up the phone. "Unknown number and probably from a burner."

Grabbing Marco's T-shirt, she looked up at him. "What is going on here?"

"Someone is watching our every move," he said as he hurried her back inside and locked the rickety handle on the door. "I'm going in to do some research on Daniel Parker and his father, Kent. Wanna join me?"

She wasn't sure, but she needed answers. "I'll meet you in the small sitting room near our rooms. So we don't wake Rosa and Alan."

"I'll be there with my laptop, after I check the whole house."

Amelia pulled at the terry cloth robe she had on over her leggings and long T-shirt, a shiver running down her body even in the summer heat. While she waited for Marco, she listened to the voice message again.

"Daniel?" she whispered. Now she wished she'd answered. She could call the number but that might be a setup of some kind to torment her even more.

Marco found her in the sitting room, the curtains drawn and only one lamp lighted. He had two bottles of water he'd snatched from the kitchen refrigerator.

He sat for a moment, his eyes holding hers. "That was amazing. The kissing part, I mean."

Amelia nodded, unable to speak. "Not so much the someone-watching-and-calling-me-to-let-me-know part."

"No, that's not so good."

She rubbed her forearms. "It's beginning to creep me out more than I want to admit."

"Okay," he said, "somehow this impersonator manages to get on the property in spite of the beefed-up security measures. I think he's got some inside help, or he knows a secret path."

Amelia gasped. "A secret path."

"Ring a bell?"

She nodded and opened her water bottle to take a long drink. "Daniel and I had a path between our properties, near the river. An old cattle lane that no one uses now." Pushing at her hair, she leaned back on the sofa. "We found it when we were fishing one day, and later, we'd sneak out to meet each other there. It's a spot by a big live oak, with rocks where we'd sit and hide. I snuck out to meet him there a lot."

"Maybe tomorrow, we should investigate this path," Marco said. "I'd like to get a feel on the Park Meadows Ranch anyway."

"We can take a ride—on horses. Easier to get there and less conspicuous."

"Good idea," he said. "And meantime, I'm going to go through all the reports again on Daniel's accident. It looks like he skidded off the road, but I'd like to know why. I'm guessing no one had ever done a thorough backtracking on that, since the reports and the newspaper articles all say the same thing."

"I never did," she admitted. "Just too painful."

"Will you be okay with this?"

"I have to do it, don't I?"

"We have to do it, to get this unfinished business out of the way, so we can finish the business we started out there under the stars."

She nodded and smiled, then a chill rushed over her when she remembered that someone had been watching them. "I can't get that voice out of my head. Daniel never talked to me like that before."

Marcus touched a hand to her hair. "It wasn't Daniel. My gut says if this man loved you the way you told me he did, he'd be beating his fist on the front door to let you know he's alive. Not lurking around outside and sending you ominous phone messages."

"You're right," she said, determination and a deep prayer for peace overtaking her fears. "I need to keep reminding myself of that, so let's get busy. And Marco, no matter what we find, you and I do have some unfinished business."

ELEVEN

An hour later, they were both tired and sleepy. But Marco now had a better understanding of Kent Parker, and he had a clear plan of how to get this done. Amelia had told him all she knew, and he'd researched the rest.

"Daniel and I were always friends, but I didn't go over to PMR a lot. Daniel's mother just up and left one day when Daniel was in high school, and she never came back. I think that made Kent a hard man to live with. I will say Daniel loved his daddy and Kent was good to him, loved him so much, obviously. But something was always off between them. Daniel and I grew close since I'd lost both my parents. And you know the rest."

"Did you ever feel Kent's resentment?"

"Not at first, because he didn't really notice us hanging out since we were usually in groups. But then when it became just Daniel and me, Kent's attitude begin to change. After Daniel told his daddy he didn't want to stay on the ranch, things got even worse. Kent began to brood and fuss at Daniel, and he implied I was a bad influence—I'd talked him into leaving the ranch. I'd never do that, but Daniel had always mentioned leaving. I think after his mother went AWOL, he wanted to just get away from the memories. But Kent blamed me and made sure I knew I wasn't welcome in his home. So Daniel started spending more time over here and he and Leo became close. That only fueled Kent's fire."

"I can see now why he'd blame all of you for Daniel's death. His wife left and now his son was planning to do the same. That had to be tough to accept."

"Yes. In his grief, he had to blame someone. He's not a believer, so he doesn't have faith to fall back on. In his mind, someone had to pay for Daniel's death."

"But that doesn't mean it was anyone's fault."

"Unless someone tried to harm Daniel on purpose."

"And Leo, too."

"I know I've fought you on your theories, but now I'm beginning to wonder."

"Let's see what we find."

Now, after reading up on Park Meadow Ranch, Marco was impressed. A small cattle ranch, it was a nice spread but not in the grandiose way of Rio Rojo. And not nearly as large and predominant. Parker's net worth was about a fourth of what Amelia had just inherited. The man had more than enough motive to want revenge on her. And possibly Leo, too.

But why? Because of Daniel's death? Why try to get his hands on property he didn't need and couldn't afford?

He could only be antagonizing Amelia, trying to scare her away, just because he wanted to hurt her. But again, she wouldn't have any reason to interact with him, so why the big production?

If he'd gone completely bitter, it would be the principle of the thing—he'd think she didn't deserve the ranch. She wasn't Leo's flesh and blood. Again, that shouldn't be Kent Parker's concern.

Marco turned from his research to ask her a question, and found her curled up on the settee, asleep. Shutting the computer, he went over and put a soft chenille throw over her. Puff had followed them into the room and now lay snuggled up on the floor beside her.

Marco sat back in a recliner and thought through every moment since he'd found her.

Someone had either tailed him to her place or had found her and shown up at the same time as him. He'd checked his truck for any tracking, and he always made sure his phone didn't track him. He'd checked her phone and this whole house for bugs. Could someone be feeding information to Kent Parker? Samuel, Ben, before he was killed, Gregory Tyson, in the hospital and silent, the kid who'd brought the photo? Someone controlled this whole thing.

He stayed there in the chair, watching Amelia sleep. Puff never left her side. The dog would be a good guard for her, too.

Marco thought about the man who was acting as Daniel. Earlier when he couldn't sleep, he'd looked up all the news articles he could find on Daniel's accident. They didn't offer much more than the general details. But he did notice in one article, the reporter made a point of saying it happened on Rio Rojo land, and that the vehicle had swerved and hit a tree head-on.

What had caused that vehicle to swerve? That was the unanswered question.

They might not ever know, but Marco had a feeling someone had done something to cause that wreck. He'd gone online to get a traffic report, paying the fee with a secure card. He planned to check with the locals again. He might find someone who was willing to talk about it more, even though superiors didn't like to let their first responders talk about such things unless they were in court. He also planned to pay Gregory Tyson another visit. The man would be released from the hospital soon and taken into custody. Marco wanted to have a chat with him before he went behind bars.

Glancing over at Amelia again, he thought about their kiss earlier. A kiss that had knocked him off his feet. His attraction to her made no sense, but that kiss had made it all fall into place. He needed her in his life. Unbelievable since he'd fought any kind of commitments for so long now, and he'd only met her a few days ago. He'd left more women angry at him than he cared to remember. Maybe it had something to do with his daddy. The man sure had made life hard on both Marco and his mother. But she was safe now and loved her life.

Why couldn't he move on from the pain of having a father who didn't love him? Amelia had abandonment issues, and understandably, and he had commitment issues.

What a pair we are.

He prayed, deeply and fiercely, for some relief from these people pursuing her. She'd done nothing wrong, and he should know. He'd learned a lot, searching for her. But she'd held out on the hurt and pain of what she'd had to endure. He also prayed for whatever seemed to be happening between them.

Lord, let this be right. Let us stay strong. Help me to put faith over fear.

On the verge of dozing off, he heard a noise coming

from Amelia's bedroom. Jumping up, Marco reached for his gun.

He'd left it in his room.

Not wanting to waste time, he grabbed a heavy decorative candleholder and headed for her room. Puff jumped up, sniffing, and followed, a low growl emitting as he went.

"C'mon, boy, let's see who's in there."

Amelia woke up with a start, her nightmare full of fire and a man holding her down. She sat up and looked around. The sitting room. Marco and Puff were gone.

Then she heard a thud and a groan coming from her room. And Puff, barking.

She shot up, stumbled, got her footing and hurried around the corner. "Marco?"

"In here," he called from her room.

Puff's bark grew more distant.

Amelia rushed in, spotting him on the floor by the open door to the courtyard. "Marco? What happened? Where's Puff?"

"You had another intruder," he said, lifting up off the floor. "He tried to fight me, and I fought back with this." He reached down and picked up a huge stone candleholder. "He hit me square in the gut, but I got in a knock to his right cheek. He left bleeding, and with Puff on his trail."

He grunted and pushed up then went to the door, Amelia behind him. "Puff?"

The dog stood at the back gate, still sniffing. But he came running when he saw Amelia.

Amelia took the candleholder and guided Marco to a chair. "Are you all right?"

"I am. But he got away before I could get in another lick."

"Did you get a good look at him?" she asked, dreading the answer.

The expression on Marco's face said it all. "I did, Amelia. And since I've spent most of the night looking at articles containing pictures of Daniel, I have to tell you the man who slugged me in the gut kind of did look like him."

Amelia sank down on the other chair and held her hands to her face. "This can't be real. If Daniel is alive, why is he trying to scare me away and harm everyone I care about? You'd think he'd come to the front door and tell me he's okay, just as you pointed out earlier."

Marco gave her a glance filled with regret and confusion. "I still don't think it's Daniel. Someone could have found a look-alike who's posing as him, though."

"Did he say anything?" she asked, her heart being stabbed with what felt like jagged glass.

"No, and he wasn't really bothering anything. Just standing inside the door, but I caught him before he had time to do anything. I grabbed the first thing I could get my hands on. Should have taken my gun. We need to call an alarm company tomorrow. We're not waiting any longer on that."

"Yes." She looked at the old latch. "It's on the list, the growing list, of things I need to do."

"He definitely got inside this room." Pointing to the double glass doors, Marco said, "The lock wasn't secure to begin with, and he pried it right open. I don't want to think about what might have happened if you'd been in here sleeping."

She didn't want to think of that, either. "I've never

worried about locking doors or adding security here. Leo didn't think about those things, either. We all felt safe here before. But I think things here have changed more than I want to accept."

"Which means someone is helping this person to torment you. We thought it was Ben Nesmith, but he's been eliminated. Someone who works on this ranch or has access to a lot of things around here is making it easy for this interloper to just walk right inside this house."

"It's like a needle in a haystack, but we've cleared most of the ranch hands. And I know Rosa and Alan can't be behind this."

"Tomorrow, we'll check with Tommy. He seems to be honest and a good worker. Ask him if anyone new was hired before Ben was killed. He'd also know who was assigned to which pastures. We'll double-check with the hired guards at the front gate. We should find some hired guards to watch out near the river, too."

"Just more to add to the mystery," she said. "I doubt I'll sleep tonight. I might not ever get a good night's rest if I live here again."

"You can sleep," Marco told her. "Puff and I will guard the door."

"And how do you plan on doing that?"

"I'll sit out there in the courtyard with my gun and your dog. Those cushioned chairs look mighty comfortable."

"No, you won't." She got up and shut the door and locked it. "I can sleep here with Puff to warn me. And you can go back to your room and leave the door open."

"I don't like that. He's long gone, but we'll have to

report this to the sheriff. Too late to get them out here now."

"Well, I'm not letting you sleep out there with lizards and mosquitoes and the heat and…someone prowling around. Tomorrow, I'm going to conduct a meeting with everyone who works here and make it clear that their watchman techniques are not working and if I find out any one of them is messing with me, and this ranch, I'll have them arrested. Then I'm going to go over and confront Kent Parker."

"Not without me."

"Then go to your room and get some sleep. I have my gun and I'll be fine. Right, Puff?"

Puff barked in agreement.

"At least we didn't wake Rosa and Alan," he said, moving toward her.

"They can't hear very well, and their apartment is on the other side of the house," she said.

"Ah, good to know. We'll need to warn them. I have some suggestions on how we might proceed, but they can wait till we start over tomorrow."

"We will. Look, we've made progress tonight." Then she turned and tugged at the heavy drapes. "Well, I thought we had. I just can't believe that could have been Daniel tonight."

"Me, either," he said. He moved one of the heavy leather chairs to the slider, wedging the chair's wooden back legs against the slider's track. "That should hold enough to warn you if he tries anything again tonight." Then he tugged her close. "I don't wish anyone dead, Amelia, but I kinda want you to myself, know what I mean?"

"I do," she replied. "I'd like that, one day, Marco."

Unable to stop herself, she pulled him close and kissed him, just so she could feel the warmth of his arms around her. "Stay safe, okay?"

Marco gazed at her, his beautiful eyes only for her, which made her feel safe and shivery all in one breath. But she'd never really be safe and free to explore her feelings for him until this was over. "You, too. I'm definitely keeping the door open and my weapon nearby."

"Thank you. Again," she said, thinking how much her life had changed because this man had found her. But she said prayers of gratitude for Marco. He was the only part of this whole weird nightmare that had kept her from screaming out in rage and pain.

He gave her a slight smile, then left her standing there with Puff. Standing there with her heart torn apart. She still loved one man, but she was fairly sure she was falling for another one. And he was alive and well and doing his best to keep her safe. If Daniel was alive, she'd have to make a tough decision. One that would change her life all over again, either way.

TWELVE

Marco woke the next day energized despite the scare they'd had last night. He'd figured out how to do what he was best at—surveillance. So much had happened, he'd had little time to form a plan. But now he had one.

He found Rosa and Alan in the kitchen, cooking breakfast as always. Those two loved doing everything together, and it showed in every gesture. He wanted that. Never had before, but now, he wanted that. To be with another person you loved reminded him of a dance with every step in sync and choreographed through habit and with a lot of hope, love and faith. He'd never seen his parents in union about anything. No wonder he had a hard time in the love department. But kissing Amelia made it all fall right into place, like a dance step you didn't know you could do. Like a sensation you'd never experienced before. Like your heart caught between hurt and hope.

"Morning," he said, rubbing his hair back off his face, and shaking those mushy thoughts right out of his head.

Rosa turned and smiled. *"Buenos dias."*

"Did you sleep well?" Alan asked as he handed Marco

a plate of scrambled eggs with chorizo, and a huge biscuit brimming with butter and blueberry jam.

"Nope. Not at all." He filled them in, watching for any odd reaction, or any sign that they'd had something to do with all this.

They were both shocked and obviously shook up. "This is terrible," Rosa said, fear and doubt in her eyes. "And cruel." Then she sat down next to Marco. "But at the funeral, the coffin was closed. Mr. Parker requested it."

"You mean Daniel's funeral?"

"*Si.* And he only allowed a few people to attend. I was surprised he allowed us to be there with Leo."

Marco made a mental note of that.

Amelia came in, pushing at her hair and yawning, Puff on her heels. "Morning."

"We heard you had a busy night," Alan said, giving her black coffee and her own biscuit.

"Too busy. Too many people around here trying to get to me in every way possible."

Marcus took a sip of coffee. "Well, last night was too close. In your room, Amelia. Which is why Alan and I are going to make sure you get better security on the house." He got up and poured himself more coffee. "So, I have a plan."

They all leaned in. "What?" Alan asked, his dark eyes trusting.

"Well, Amelia, you have the perfect weapon to use in this case and it's not a gun or a candleholder. It's your camera."

She put down her cup. "I haven't even thought about taking pictures, Marco. Been a little distracted."

"Exactly. But what better weapon to use when we're doing a stakeout today and maybe even tonight."

Her expression changed as realization hit her. "You're right. Good idea. I have a great zoom lens on that thing. And I have a smaller camera for when I just need to take photos for inspiration."

Rosa grinned. "You can have proof, good or bad, *si*?"

"Si," Amelia replied, smiling. A beautiful sight. "After I have a meeting with the entire staff, we can snoop around. I need to get the lay of the land."

Marco nodded. "An understatement. We'll take the horses and supplies and camp out if we need to, as we'd planned last night, and see how people are getting onto the ranch from the river. And we'll find out if any path leads back to Park Meadows."

"That could work." She sliced her biscuit in half and slathered it with butter. "Most of our land is fenced all the way down to the river, but there are always ways to get around fences."

Marco saw the resolve in her eyes and wondered about the fences around her heart. "That is a true statement."

"Okay," Amelia said, after draining her coffee. "I'm going to have a long talk with the ranch workers. They're reporting in with nothing. How can they miss someone walking right into my room?"

"Be careful," Marco said. "I'm going to find out more from Gregory Tyson. I found out he's been taken to the county jail, so that means he's recovered from his wounds."

"I'll go with Amelia," Alan offered. "Then I'll start calling security companies."

"Rosa, I need you to do something for us, too," Marco said.

Rosa nodded. "Of course."

THIRTEEN

Amelia and Marco decided to wait on going into Siri's studio. It was getting late, but they got on their way to ride the river, and kept their excursion slow and easy, talking quietly in case anyone was following them. Amelia had always loved riding her horse around the ranch. She and Daniel would meet up in the back forty and have picnics, talk about the future and enjoy the stark beauty of the land around them.

Those memories held steady as the sun beamed down on them and dragonflies buzzed around, fluttering through the bluebonnets and red poppies. Spring in the Hill Country was always surprising. A lone oak tree could be standing by an aged tractor. A wagon wheel could show up along a crooked, broken fence line, sunflowers blooming all around.

Right now, the wind picked up and lifted the wildflowers, making the fields and pastures look like a giant floating quilt.

The river gurgled and changed as they moved higher through the hills, ever changing and always on the move, tiny waterfalls following a path to forever.

"I'd forgotten how beautiful it is here in the spring," Amelia said, acutely alert that they could be shot at.

"It is pretty," Marco said, keeping his roan close to her rambunctious Buster. "But be aware." He shifted on the saddle and did a scan. "This might not be the best idea. We're inviting trouble."

"Do you think someone is following us?"

"Not yet, but I should be keeping you under lock and key, not taking a ride out in the wide open."

"I needed this," she said. "And Alan put two new men on us, remember?"

"Yeah, they're being discreet but I'm glad they're back there."

"Okay, so we're being extra careful, and we've got a plan, so pretend we're just out for a ride."

While her heart bumped and beat warnings left and right. Warnings about her tormentors, and warnings about the man who rode beside her. She shouldn't ignore those warnings, but here she was.

They moved over a few hills and then went down toward the river, an old trail leading the way. "This is where Leo and Siri loved to come and spend the day. I guess his ashes are out here while he's now with her up there in those puffy clouds."

"They had a good life together," Marco stated. "A once-in-a-lifetime kind of life from what I've heard."

"I never saw them fight," she replied. "Always smiling and together. She loved art and he loved to take pictures. He did change after she passed away. His heart was broken, but he was still a kind, loving man."

"I'm sorry I never met him," Marco said. "We should still check out her studio, too. Never know what a picture or a painting can tell you."

"Well, we've tried everything else," she said. "Let's pull up by that big oak near the river."

He did as she said, leading the way to the huge live oak that served like a massive umbrella hanging over the shallow waters and chunky rocks. She stopped here and there, taking random shots, remembering how much she loved her work.

"I get the feeling I'm not the first person who's been here with you," Marco said, glancing around.

"I've been here many times, with many people. It's a great photo op."

"That it is," he said, his eyes sweeping over her.

"You can't do that," she said.

"Do what?"

"That eye thing, the way you look at me."

"I like looking at you, which is strange since I usually don't ogle my clients, let alone kiss my clients."

She put her hands on her hips. "I'm technically not your client."

He unpacked their supplies and spread out a blanket. "Samuel is keeping a running tab."

"But he hired you, so that's his problem."

"Okay, then, I like looking at you." He looped the roan's bridle around a sapling branch and turned to her. "I'm watching, Amelia. We need to pretend we're enjoying ourselves, but not happy-happy. You know."

"Oh, because people are dying around here and about ten other things to deal with. Trust me, I'm not happy."

"Got it." They settled on the blanket and had some water and brownies Rosa has slipped in their saddlebags. "Now that we're here, can you remember any secret trails between the two properties? You know, places most wouldn't see or know about?"

"Only the one Daniel and I used."

"Is that one going to stay a secret?"

"No. It's not far from here."

Amelia had her camera out, taking shots of the water and the old oak—her favorite tree on the place. She'd usually come here alone until Daniel. Everything about her favorite places on the ranch had changed after that. Had he been here recently?

Wouldn't she feel something if he'd been here?

She glanced around, the chill of realization making her shiver in the warm wind. "It's been a while since I've traveled this far from the house, of course. The river narrows right around this bend, separates the two properties and then we have streams and tributaries that finger out in both directions."

Thinking about how she and several friends, including Daniel, had explored just about every inch of the land and the river, she didn't speak about her memories out loud. It didn't seem proper to keep remembering one man, when another one was sitting here with her, his eyes never venturing far away.

She stopped, lowering her head. What was she doing here? Fighting for the truth? Or trying to forget all the pain? Could she let go and find comfort with Marco?

"I need to think," she admitted. "I need to remember."

Finally, a dim image popped into her head. "Caverns, caves, maybe. I remember finding a small cave that was so scary, some of the girls refused to go in it."

"But you did?" he asked with a firm tone.

"Only once and I told myself I'd never go in there again. I can't remember where exactly, but I think it was hidden in some rocks between the properties near a stream to the east."

"Then east we head," he replied, giving her a smile that shouted be careful. "Keep that camera handy."

They followed the curve in the river, bees humming in their ears, butterflies hovering over the bluebonnets. The world seemed so far away out here. Marco wished this could be a normal day with a beautiful woman, but this was anything but normal.

He couldn't relax. He couldn't fall for her.

"Marco?"

Shaking off his regrets, Marco glanced to where she pointed. "I think that's it." She squinted into the sun. "Daniel and I used to walk beyond this cave to another path. But I don't even see the entrance to that one anymore. If someone wanted a quicker way to get onto the Triple R, this spot would be it."

They trotted along in the shallows, the water slashing up behind them. He studied the rock formation that split the streambed in half.

"It's like a natural tunnel," he said, taking in what looked to be about an eight-foot rock formation hunching over the water before it dropped beyond the stream. "Are you telling me this rock wall goes down on one side?"

"If I remember correctly," she said. "I didn't linger in there last time."

"And you were with him?"

Daniel.

She nodded, her gaze holding steady. "I can't lie about it. Yes. I was with him a lot in these hills, Marco. But he's not here now."

"Oh, he's still here, all around. He's not alive, but he's here. I can see it in your eyes."

"And that makes you angry?"

"No. I have no hold over any of this, or over you. I get it—you loved him, and he died. That's cruel and unfair. And now someone's using your love for Daniel to taunt you and play tricks with your mind."

"So what are you saying?"

Marco let out a sigh while he studied the rocks, thinking this big one that split the river was kind of like the wall between her and him. She'd already been way out of his league the night he met her. Now, she owned all of this, and she still longed for another man to rule this kingdom with her.

"I'm saying let's get this done. Find these people and end that suffering at least."

"You mean, me thinking I see Daniel and when I don't see him, still thinking about him?"

"Yes, Amelia. But mostly, I want you to feel safe and stay alive. The rest will be figured out after I've accomplished that goal."

Her eyes held hurt and confusion while she set her expression to a stony neutral. "Then let's get into that cave before the sun goes down."

He followed her around the big rock, wondering why he'd been so blunt in his feelings. Maybe because he'd never had such feelings before.

Focus. He asked God to give him a focused mind and the ability to make wise decisions.

Amelia pointed to a low-hanging tree limb. "This hasn't changed that much. The tree's bigger and the limb is hiding the cave even more."

They tied off the horses, then Marco pulled out a

small, high-powered flashlight. "Are you sure there's a cave in there?"

"Yes," she replied in a clipped voice, her frustration and anger palpable. "I can't believe I'd almost forgotten something like that."

And she couldn't almost forget Daniel, he thought. And that was that.

"Well, you're right. This is definitely a cave," Marco said as they made their way through the narrow formation. "If the river ever floods, this will be under way pretty quickly."

"We rarely have floods," she said, her firm tone echoing through the damp walls. "But yes, I could see that happening."

Still burning from his words to her earlier, Amelia wondered again how she expected a good outcome with any of this. Being in this cave with Marco only clarified how much danger she was in. And it also clarified how much she'd come to like and appreciate him. "I don't want to die, Marco," she said.

"We all die, Amelia, but I won't let that happen to you anytime soon."

"But how can I live here with someone constantly trying to scare me away?"

"You live by faith, right?"

"Yes." She'd certainly lived her faith after losing most of the people she loved. She'd prayed about finding someone who wouldn't leave her or die on her. And yet, here she was, wishing for time with Marco. Would he leave, too? She couldn't take that chance again. She moved to get out of the cave.

He nudged her back to reality. "And you've shown me how to do the same, right? Live by faith?"

"I've tried. Even now I know God has plans for me. Maybe for us."

"Yes. I've prayed more this week than I have in five years."

"But you're angry about all of this. I've messed with your plans to take the money you're owed…and run."

"Plans can change, darling." He glanced back at her. "And I wasn't trying to run. Go, yes, run, no. I have things I want to get done and over."

She figured he wasn't scared of anything much, but maybe a commitment. She didn't want that, either, did she?

Reminding herself that he'd been with her through all of this, she also wished he'd never had to show up at her door. That she'd never inherited anything, and she could keep her simple life on Caddo Lake, taking pictures of the stark beauty there, and enjoying doing family photos and pictures with Santa on the side.

They heard scuffling, like a rodent was running away. Amelia shivered. "Snakes?"

"I don't see any. Probably a squirrel." Marco stopped and shined the light in an area that widened, causing her to blink. "Look, Amelia."

She moved close, the warmth of his T-shirt making her feel safe. "What?"

"Footprints," he said. "Fresh ones. Proof that someone has been coming and going between the two properties. And recently, too. It's just muddy enough in here to give a good boot print."

"This means they've been avoiding any fences or security restrictions," she said. "This is where the two ranches merge together back on land. A clear line in the sand, so to speak, and at the end of both properties where the river splits off. The last place anyone would think of using."

"Anyone except a deliberate intruder," Marco said. "Easy passageway between the two properties and access to the other side of the river."

"And they could move over almost all of the ranch once there."

"Yep. For a big spread, the Triple R doesn't have the best of security." He tugged her around the muddy footprints after she'd taken some photos. "Let's see what we can find before full dark."

Amelia tried to breathe deeply, but this tight dark place gave her a sinking feeling, a feeling of defeat. The facts of her situation weren't lost on her. Someone was after her.

When they reached the other side, she gasped for air the minute she saw the narrow opening leading back into the rocks and woods. "That wasn't any fun."

"Well, we have to go back that way."

"Do you see anything or anyone?"

Marco scanned the horizon all around. "I see a trail through the grass, a worn-down one. Someone's been coming this way for a while now and I think they're using an off-road vehicle of some kind. See those tire tracks?"

They checked around the cave. "This is Parkview property," she said. "So we can establish this person is coming from that ranch."

They didn't find anything else, but she got some good photos. Would pictures help her case, hold up in court?

Marco nodded, his gaze on the distant trees. "Yes, a breakthrough that might help us a lot."

When he heard a motor cranking off in the distance, he pivoted and shoved her back into the cave. "And I was right. Let's get back to our side and move the horses down the way a bit. Tonight, I'll watch and see who comes out of this cave and onto Triple R land."

"And hopefully, we'll finally find the truth about Daniel."

He didn't have a response to that, she noted.

By the time they made it back to the other side, darkness was falling, and a deep golden sunset hovered like a slow fire over the tree line. Amelia snapped pictures, thinking she'd have this memory, no matter what. New memories to replace old ones.

If she could live to tell about it.

FOURTEEN

Night came in vivid blue and bright orange, merging together like paint thrown onto a canvas. Amelia shivered, even though the night was warm, and bugs buzzed around the tent they'd set up.

After securing the horses in a copse of trees halfway back to the ranch, they'd pitched camp near the water, the gurgling sounds of the river soothing, while Amelia's nerves did a dance of frustration and fear. A stalker coming in the night to her room, people dying, her home constantly on watch. How could she ever get past how her life had changed so suddenly?

Glad she had gone into action and Marco was willing to help her, she thanked God for the people around her who truly cared about her. Her parents and Leo had cared. Siri had cared. Daniel had cared. And they were all dead now. She didn't want that to happen to Rosa and Alan, or to Marco.

Her hurt and grief ran deep, starting with losing her parents and then everything that had followed. She should be mad at God, but Rosa had always told her, "God loves you. That love covers a lot. That love answers your pain with hope, that love gives you what you need when you don't even know you need it."

God had given her so many things. A good home after her parents died, people who wanted the best for her, and her little cabin on Caddo Lake. She longed to be back there.

But first, this had to be done.

She watched as Marco stoked the fire and then brought her a roast beef sandwich from the cooler. "Want me to warm this on the fire?" he asked, his tone just above a whisper.

They'd been tentative with each other since the discussion they'd had about Daniel. Marco was right. Daniel was still here. Her memories only reminded her of that even more now.

"No. I'm so hungry, I'll eat it cold." She hadn't been eating enough and even her old clothes from a few years ago were loose against her skin. But tonight, she had a heightened nervous energy that needed to go away. Stress eating might help that. She took the wrapped sandwich and opened it, happy to see Rosa had filled it with cheese and spinach trimmings.

"I haven't done this in a long time," Marco said after they finished the quick meal. He sat down with her on the blanket next to their bedrolls. "I'd forgotten how many stars are in the sky."

"Me, too," she admitted. She almost said she and Daniel used to lie on a blanket and stare at the stars. "It's a big sky out here."

"Yes, and a big land to go with it."

Amelia could smell the scents of water and earth merging in a musky sweet stream, she could smell the pines, the pasture grasses, and she could hear the owls hooting, the nocturnal creatures scurrying around. "So much land. I don't know if I'm cut out to run a ranch."

"You could hire help to run it. Just be here and oversee things. You could still be a photographer, doing your thing."

"Says the man who wants to *not* be here."

"I never said that."

"But Marco, you have your own dreams, yet here you are."

"I just want the land I grew up on to…mean something."

"And what would it mean?"

He turned to her, his eyes widening. "I guess it would mean I'm somebody."

Amelia reached her hand out to him. "You are somebody. *Mi protector.*"

Then she kissed him, letting him know how much he meant to her, wanting him to know he was more than somebody. He was one of the good guys. Surprised, she accepted how he'd touched her heart in ways she'd never thought anyone could. Not even Daniel.

That thought sobered her enough to make her draw back. Before she could explain, Marco hopped up and grabbed his gun.

"Shh." He motioned to the left down the river a way. "Someone is coming. Hear that?"

"A motor?"

Marco lifted his head. "Yes, from the other side of the water. He must have that hidden somewhere. And we heard that same noise earlier." He stood and grabbed the night binoculars he'd brought. "We need to follow him on foot. He'll probably drive that thing through the cave. Just enough room. Then he'll hide it on our side of the river."

Amelia quickly grabbed her camera and got moving, glad they'd made camp behind some rocks and trees. The horses would get jittery, though, if they got a whiff of trouble.

Marco held her behind the rock as they listened. The roar of the motor sounded closer and then went silent. They waited, her hand on his arm for what seemed like hours. But minutes later they saw a man slowly moving on foot across the trail a few yards away. She didn't dare breathe, but she zoomed in on the man slinking through the night, her camera clicking. The moonlight provided enough light that she could see his face. And when she did, despite the muted light, she almost screamed.

Dropping her camera onto the grassy spot near the rocks, she turned to Marco, unable to tell him the man she'd just seen up close looked exactly like Daniel.

Marco gave her a curious glance. "We need to follow him. On foot."

She nodded, still unable to talk. Daniel? Alive. It didn't make sense to her. Somehow, she'd find a way to talk to him and ask what he was doing here.

But how?

"Amelia?"

She came out of her fog and grabbed her camera. "The man who looks like Daniel. It was him. I snapped a picture of him."

Marco handed her the camera. "Are you sure?"

"It doesn't matter. Let's follow him."

They left their sleeping bags and Marco quickly secured the horses. "Let's stay in the trees and far behind."

Amelia kept her eyes on the man in the shadows. "What if he hears us?"

"He won't."

She kept searching ahead. "He's headed for the house again."

"Alan has guards at the gate of the courtyard, and these are professionals who came from the city. The two who followed us. I called them and now they're back at the ranch."

"Will they shoot him?"

"Alan told them to detain him if they see him."

Relief washed through her. She shouldn't feel this way, but she wanted to see this man, face-to-face.

"We need to question him, not kill him," Marco said, as if reading her mind.

"Yes, a good idea."

The man kept moving through the hilly pasture, never glancing back, never stopping to rest or listen. If he knew they were there, he wasn't showing it.

Marco halted again and called ahead again, alerting Alan. "Tell the guards to be aware."

Alan mumbled and ended the call.

"Now we wait," Marco said a few minutes later as they found a hiding spot behind a big live oak. "The guards should nab him this time."

While they waited, Amelia took a deep breath, her hopes and prayers centered on what would come next. If that man was Daniel, he'd need to explain this cat-and-mouse stuff to her. If he wasn't Daniel, she'd probably scratch his eyes out.

Either way, she needed to know. She'd need closure, and then she'd have another decision to make. What she should do about Marco.

Gunshots fired, echoing out over the night.

Marco and Amelia stood and ran back to their hidden horses.

Marco had his gun ready.

"I guess the guards found him," she said as they galloped toward the house.

Marco nodded. "But why are they shooting?" He'd told Alan to hold the man, not shoot at him.

They made it to the stables and slid off their horses. Tommy came running from his apartment, wide awake now.

"Tommy, tend to the horses. I'll be back soon."

Tommy nodded, rubbing his hair back off his face. "Who's shooting?"

"We don't know," Marco shouted. "Just stay put and alert the others."

He didn't like this, and he hoped the man would still be alive when they got there.

But what they found only added to their woes. One guard down and the other standing there with his gun pointed in the direction of the river.

"What happened?" Marco asked Alan.

Alan looked from him to the guard with the gun.

"He spotted our men and shot one of them during a scuffle."

Amelia checked on the wounded man. "He needs a doctor."

"Called an ambulance already," Alan replied. "But it's a through-and-through bullet wound."

"I'm okay. Just burning in my shoulder," the man

said. "He ambushed us and took both of us down. Swift and mean, that one."

The other guard nodded. "I got in a shot but missed because he kicked the gun right out of my hand. He took off running after that."

"Did anyone get a good look at him?" Amelia asked.

Rosa came running out of the house. "I did. And he looked like Daniel. I'm sorry, but that's the truth. He was the spitting image of Daniel."

"She spotted him," Alan said. "By the time I got here, these two didn't know what hit 'em."

"We tried, Amelia," the standing guard said. "But whoever that is, he means business."

Amelia let out a huff of a sigh. "That's it. We put off confronting Kent Parker, but first thing tomorrow I'm going to talk to the man. He might not even know someone pretending to be Daniel is lurking about. I can show him the pictures I took of the man up close. I'm going to download them on my laptop and see if I can clean them up."

"Kent might know, and he could be behind all of this," Alan replied. "I can't see it, but I'm beginning to wonder."

"All the more reason to get some answers from him," Amelia said, her eyes flashing like fire.

"You're not going without me," Marco said as a siren sounded up the lane. "Before we do that, I'm getting a security company out here."

He glanced at Amelia. Her expression told him she didn't think security would help here. And he had to agree. This had turned into a stalking situation, a harassment situation and a murder case. He'd talk to the sheriff's office again tomorrow, too. "I'll have the sheriff meet us at his place, so we have a witness to our questions. He might have some of his own."

"I'm ready." Amelia stood and shook her head. "This ends, one way or another."

"We'd better get inside," Marco said, knowing she'd go rogue on him if he didn't watch out. "It's gonna be a busy day tomorrow."

But he had to wonder—how long could this go on without someone else getting killed? He held his gaze on Amelia. He wasn't about to let that happen again.

"I'm going to check on Tommy and make sure our horses were taken care of," she said. "I doubt I'll get any sleep tonight, either."

Marco fell in step beside her. "I'm sorry."

"For what?" she asked.

"For not getting him this time."

"Marco, you've done everything you could. This person knows this ranch, knows the secret places. He thinks he knows me, but Daniel would never do this. This man is evil. A possible murderer. That's not my Daniel."

"No, that doesn't sound like a man you'd fall for," he said, his heart burning to be the kind of man she'd love.

But her Daniel was still there between them.

FIFTEEN

No one in the employee apartments had seen the man. Amelia was disappointed, but that made sense because the stables were about a fourth of mile from the main house. The guards at the front gate hadn't had any episodes. That also made sense. The man was coming across the river through the cave located on the back of the property, an easy spot where he could hide if anyone stayed near the river looking for him.

But the properties met back up beyond the cave.

Amelia hadn't taken Marco that far, and now she wished she had. Only she and Daniel knew about this particular spot where the river did a quick curve and dwindled into a five-foot-wide creek bed before it picked up speed again and branched off into two smaller tributaries. That point was the closest the Parker ranch came to the Triple R, but it wasn't fenced like most of the pastures. It had always been a nonissue—just a path between the two properties in the back woods thick with mesquite trees and twisted old live oaks mixed with aged cedars carpeted in paintbrush, bluebonnets and bluestem. No one ever went back there unless they were hunting or fishing.

But she and Daniel had found an oval rock just beyond the curve that looked like a bench. That became their place. Close to the river, but private and secluded behind a huge oak, and a spread of cedars near some large yucca plants.

Amelia lay in her bed, her eyes wide open, Puff on the floor beside her. They'd left him home earlier so he wouldn't bark, but now she was glad she had the dog with her. Alan had also found a sturdy piece of wood and wedged it against the glass sliding doors, and he and Marco had put a heavy lock on the door's latch. It would be impossible, even if they could break the lock, for anyone to push the door open. That tough wood was a solid latch, and the new lock was strong, at least for now.

After she'd talked Marco into getting some sleep, she tried to do the same. If the man called her again, she'd pretend she believed he was Daniel. She'd ask him what he wanted and why he hadn't let her know he was alive. Then she'd tell him to meet her at their secret place.

If he knew where that was, she'd have her answer. If he didn't respond correctly, she'd tell him to meet her at the cave, and let him think that was their place.

She'd take her gun, of course. And somehow, she'd either shoot him enough to maim him and march him back to the ranch, or she'd at least know the truth and send the authorities after him if he got away. But she'd also take her camera and set it up on the small tripod she kept handy. She could hide it in a tree and go back for it later. If things went wrong, maybe someone would find the camera there and see the evidence.

It was a risky plan, which is why she couldn't tell Marco about it. But then, she'd always fought her own battles. She'd fought for Daniel's love, even when his father tried to stop her. She'd fought for her career even when it had taken her to dangerous places. And she always, always fought for the truth.

Could Kent Parker really be the one harassing her? Would he deliberately hire someone to gaslight her and intimidate her?

She had to find out. If Parker wouldn't come clean, she'd keep digging with or without Marco.

She wanted to be with Marco, to know him completely and explore the bond that had brought them together, but she had to do this on her own. Because if Daniel was truly alive and tormenting her, she had to understand why.

She lay listening to the house creaking, to the wind dancing through the wind chimes in the courtyard, to the sounds of night animals roaming outside. Finally she dozed, her dreams a mixture of the past and the present. A man walked toward her, his hand reaching for her. Daniel.

But when the man came close and smiled, it wasn't Daniel.

Marco took her hand and led her away, while Daniel called her name, begging her to stay.

She woke up in a cold sweat and sat up to stare into the darkness. Alan and Marco had posted patrols all along the river.

She had to be safe tonight. She stood and pulled on her robe, then opened her door to head to the kitchen.

And found Marco sitting up against the wall, his head bent in sleep. He must have been guarding her door, waiting to hear any noise coming from her room.

Amelia sank down beside him, causing him to lift his head and go on alert.

She took his hand. "It's just me, Marco. The woman who's brought you so much trouble."

"Are you all right?" he asked, his voice husky from sleep, his hair tumbled and wild. "Did you hear something?"

"I didn't hear anything. And right now, yes, I'm okay."

His tense expression crumbled into a wry smile. "Then I can handle the trouble."

"I have no doubt, but I wish you didn't have to do that." She pulled him into her arms and held him. "I had a bad dream, but the ending was kind of nice."

"Oh, yeah?"

"Yeah. You were there at the end."

He whispered in her ear. "I can always be there if you'd like."

"I might like that once I know you won't get yourself killed on my account."

Puff came running out, sniffing the air.

Then he sniffed Marco's hand and plopped down beside them.

"This sure beats camping out," Marco said, his kiss moving through her hair.

"You got that right."

They sat there for a while, silent and still, holding on to each other until she finally said, "I think I might sleep now. How about you?"

He nodded. "My back isn't happy."

"Go get in your real bed and try to relax."

"I'm not so good at relaxing."

"Marco, go."

"I'm leaving my door open, just in case," he said,

his finger trailing down her cheek with a warm whisper against her skin.

"Tomorrow," she replied. "We'll get back on it tomorrow."

He smiled at her. "You know, we need to go on a date one day."

"That's the plan, cowboy."

She smiled and shut her door.

A date would be so nice and normal.

But she had a lot to get through before putting on a pretty dress and going on a date with Marco.

Early the next morning, Marco and Alan met with the security team and went over the whole house. It would take a lot of time and money to get what they needed, but Amelia agreed the company could get started. Marco had vetted them and recommended them, and Alan had gone over the details and agreed.

So that would be starting next week. Had they really been here almost a whole week? Seemed to Marco, something new and bad developed with each day. It would get worse. The harassment would escalate.

But last night. Nothing else had happened last night once the man had gotten away, so their aggressive measures were paying off. He'd made some more calls regarding Leo's health, but neither the medical examiner nor the hospital could tell him much. Now he had to believe someone had poisoned Leo. Could that be part of what Tyson had hinted at?

Last night had brought the dangerous too close again.

Last night. Amelia in his arms, holding him tight. Why did that feel perfect? Perfect in the midst of mayhem and tension.

Would that adrenaline rush die down once this was over and she was free and clear? Or would she find Daniel alive and well and willing to pick up where they left off? Was he afraid, so he'd gone to desperate measures to get her back here?

"What are you thinking about?" she asked after they'd had breakfast. She grabbed her tote as they headed out the door, her bracelet slipping down her arm in a jingly melody.

"Everything," he admitted. "I haven't heard from Chastain on the money trail in New Mexico. He said it might take a few days. Think he's stalling?"

She shook her head. "I think Samuel is the real deal. He's been around since I was kid, Marco. He loved Leo and Siri, and always did right by them. He wouldn't betray Leo now."

"I'm still keeping an eye on him."

"You can't keep an eye on everyone all the time."

"It's habit," he admitted. "When you grow up with an alcoholic, you learn to take charge."

Amelia nodded, but thankfully didn't send him a look of pity. He'd made peace with his past and as long as his mom was safe, Marco could live with that.

"Are you ready to talk to Kent Parker?" he asked as they walked toward his truck.

"Yes, and Samuel is supposed to meet us there."

They drove toward the road in silence, then Amelia said, "I can show you the spot where Daniel went off the road."

"So you got there pretty quickly after it happened?"

"Yes. I ran all the way, but by the time I arrived a fire truck had already arrived." She took a deep breath.

"They put out the flames, but his truck was…completely gone."

She inhaled a breath. "I called out for him, searched all around. Then one of the firemen told me he…he hadn't survived."

"Amelia, I know this is hard, but did you see them taking away Daniel's body?"

She put a hand to her mouth. "No—Leo dragged me away." Then she turned in the seat. "Leo dragged me away, Marco. I don't remember much after that."

"Okay, who else was there that you remember?"

She closed her eyes. "I've tried so hard to forget. I don't know. Several firemen, sheriff's deputies, EMTs."

"Think. Could anyone there have been an outsider, someone who'd come back to admire his work?"

Amelia opened her eyes. "How could anyone do something like that?"

"I'm sorry," he said, hating to put her through this. "But the mind is good at playing tricks on us, and people can be as good when they're playing tricks."

Amelia closed her eyes again and then as they reached the curve she'd mentioned several times, she opened her eyes and said, "I did mention *someone* else being there that night. The man I thought looked like Daniel, remember?"

"I'm listening," he said as he pulled the truck off the road and then gave her his full attention.

Amelia glanced around, taking in the changes since she'd been here. The trees were tall and willowy, and the roadside had thickets here and there. "This is different." Then she opened the door and got out, her eyes scanning the area where Daniel's truck had crashed into a tree and exploded.

Marco hopped out and came around the front of the truck to meet her. He didn't speak. He let her absorb the memories and the pain of that night.

"The tree," she said, walking to the right. "It's covered with brush, but it should still have a scar."

She pointed and started pulling away brambles near a massive old live oak. Marco did the same, then he pulled back. "Is this the place?"

Amelia's expression said it all. Her eyes watered, her hand went to her mouth. She turned and held her arms on the truck, her head going down. "Yes."

Marco came behind her and put his arms around her waist. "I'm sorry."

He hurt because she hurt. She had loved this man completely. He wanted to be jealous, but how could he? Daniel sounded like the perfect man—a doctor who cared about those in need, a son who wanted to break out on his own, a man who now couldn't defend himself. Marco couldn't compete with that.

She lifted her head and turned to face him as he stood back. "Someone else was here, but like I said, I thought I was imagining things. I remember glancing back toward the ranch, searching for anyone to tell me how this happened. And for a split second, I thought I saw Daniel walking away. I can see it so clearly now that I'm back here."

"But it wasn't him?"

She shook her head. "I called out his name, but everyone thought I was still in shock. I ran toward the darkness, shouting, but Leo stopped me. I looked back, but the man was gone."

"His back was to you?"

"Yes, but he walked like Daniel. I think I wanted it to be him. Just like I want it to be him now."

"Did anyone see the man?"

"I called out several times, but Leo told me again that Daniel was gone. Then Kent showed up in a rage, telling me this was my fault. Leo and he almost got into a fight, so Leo took me home and gave me some of his sleeping pills to calm me. I still had horrible nightmares. Still to this day."

She moved in a circle, her gaze checking both sides of the road. "But somehow, I'd blocked that out. Seeing that man. I think I decided it had all been in my imagination, even when I mentioned him to you before. But now—"

"Now you have to wonder?"

"Let's go and talk to Parker. I need something solid to get me over this notion of Daniel being back."

"Amen to that."

They got back in the truck, but Amelia turned and looked back until they were around the curve, until the jagged, scarred tree was out of sight.

SIXTEEN

The Park Meadows Ranch house was a two-story white farmhouse style, rambling and surrounded by porches and huge, towering live oaks. The grounds were cultivated with old-growth azaleas just beginning to bloom in vivid pinks and lush oranges and reds.

Marco took it all in, thinking this was amazingly different from the more Southwestern style of the Rio Rojo, smaller and more traditional, less intriguing, not as historic.

But it would do in a pinch, and they were in a pinch to talk to Kent Parker.

So they got out of the truck, Amelia looking as if she might bolt any minute.

"I could have done this without you," he said.

"No, my problem, my confrontation."

"Have you always been this stubborn?"

She wiped her hands down her worn jeans. "Pretty much."

He followed her up the brick steps to the wide front porch with a sky-blue ceiling and gray planked floors. Two big white rocking chairs graced the right side, a matching table with a geranium flowering red between them. On the left side, an intricate wooden bench was centered between two huge parlor ferns.

"So serene."

"So a facade."

He could believe that. "And he lives here alone?"

"As far as I know."

He rang the doorbell, noting how the place looked deserted and empty. Since no one from the Triple R had much to do with this property, it was hard to tell if anyone was here.

No one came to the door.

"He could be away on business," she said, doing a scan of the front yard and the sloping side yards. "Let's go around back. Maybe a housekeeper is here, at least."

They strolled around, Marco glancing into windows as they went. The place appeared open and airy, but they couldn't find anyone.

Amelia went up on the back porch and peered into the kitchen. "Marco, look at the table."

Marco glanced in. "A cup of coffee and a plate of toast and half-eaten bacon."

"Somebody doesn't want to talk to us."

"Is Parker this shy all the time?"

"No. I would think he'd take pride in confronting me."

"So could someone else be staying here?"

"I have no idea."

They heard a car pulling in. "Let's hope that's Parker."

They hurried back around the corner. Marco noticed the stables down a trail to the left, but he didn't see any action there, either.

Samuel Chastain's sleek BMW slid up the drive.

He got out, dressed as usual in a nice suit and a white cowboy hat.

"I just got news," he said, out of breath.

"Talk to me," Amelia replied, her eyes still darting here and there in a search for answers.

"First, Kent Parker is not home. I finally reached a caretaker who lives somewhere on the property. He said Kent had business in another state."

"Do we know where he went?" Marco asked.

Samuel lowered his voice. "I did some asking around and found out."

"Okay, tell us." Amelia's nerves rattled against her bones.

"New Mexico," Samuel explained. "To see his ex-wife."

"What?" Amelia shook her head. "He always said he didn't know where she was. Daniel tried to find out, but he couldn't locate her, either."

Samuel took off his hat and shook it against his leg. "Well, his daddy knows where she is now, and maybe he's known all along. What we didn't know, and what he might now know, is that Leo knew where she was, too, and was sending her money."

"That's where the five K a month was going?" Amelia asked, her eyes wide.

"Yes," Samuel said. "And I knew nothing about it. So Leo had some secrets." He shook his head and did his own scan. "I'm getting a bad feeling, standing here."

A second later, gunshots rang out, spraying bullets all around them.

"Get down," Marco said, reaching for his gun. Amelia got behind Samuel's car, crouching against the tire on the driver's side.

"Where are they coming from?"

"The stables from what I can tell," Marco said. "I guess they were waiting for a good line of fire."

"They found it," Samuel said. "I think they pinged my car."

"Forget the car," Marco said, crouching toward the front to get a bead on the shooter. "We've got to find better cover."

Amelia watched, her heart dropping. "So what's the plan?"

"I'll distract them," Marco said. "Samuel, your job is to get Amelia away from here."

"To where?" Samuel asked. "I see trees and a locked house."

"Get her to the porch and around the other corner."

"And you'll cover us?" Samuel asked with a squeak.

"Yes," Marco said. "Hey, I was a sniper. Army Rangers."

Samuel let out a sigh. "Oh, okay, then. Good to know."

"On three, you two head for the trees to the left and make your way back to the house."

Amelia wasn't sure she could do this—leave him shooting and possibly getting hit? "Are you going to be okay?"

"Amelia, you know what you're doing, and I know what I need to do. You and Samuel get to a safe spot. I'll take care of the rest."

Samuel nodded. "Oh, by the way I have a high-powered rifle in the trunk. Loaded."

Marco frowned as another shot hit the trees. "You could have led with that."

"I was a tad distracted."

"Pop the trunk."

Samuel jingled his key fob and the trunk unlocked but didn't lift. Amelia breathed a sigh of relief.

Then she said, "Give me your handgun, Marco. I'll cover you until you can get the rifle."

"No."

"Yes."

He handed her the gun with a reluctant grunt. "When I raise the trunk, you start shooting. The bullets won't go far, but they don't know that."

Amelia duck-walked to the front of the car.

Marco slipped to the trunk. The minute he opened it a couple of inches, shots sparked around them. Amelia fired back, knocking off several rounds.

Marco lifted the trunk, slid close to get his hand on the rifle and peeled it out while shots volleyed back and forth. One of the passenger windows shattered, causing Samuel to moan.

Then Marco hit the ground, checked the rifle and tested the scope. After moving it back and forth, he spotted someone through a window high up in what looked like a loft apartment. "I see a dark beanie hat in the stable loft."

"Hit it," Amelia suggested after watching him, tired of this.

Marco got on the ground and aimed the rifle, his eye squinting through the scope, while Amelia watched and prayed.

Marco had the shooter in his sights.
But the man pulled off his cap.
Marco hesitated and looked again.
"It's our man," he said. "The Daniel doppelgänger."

Amelia tugged away from Samuel and hurried back. "What?"

"Our shooter is the man we've been spotting all over the ranch. I think he might be a squatter in the hayloft while Parker is away. Probably enjoying breakfast in the main house until we showed up."

"Don't shoot him," she said.

Marco didn't take his eyes off the man. "And why not?"

Samuel scooted back. "I thought I was escorting you to a safe place, Amelia. We need to get to the house for cover."

"It's the man," she said. "The one harassing me."

"Yeah, well, he's doing a good job of it right now," Samuel replied. "And I have a cramp in my left leg, just above my boot."

Marco scoped the man again. "He seems to be waiting, watching, taunting us maybe?"

"Just shoot into the air near him," Amelia said, her voice strained. "I don't want him dead. I need answers."

Marco shook his head. "Amelia, go with Samuel to the house. I can cover y'all now that I have this rifle, and maybe get him off that perch so I can corner him."

Silence.

"Amelia?"

"I'll go, but Marco, don't kill him."

The plea came from her heart. She'd let this man get away with murder and go back to him? If he really was Daniel coming back to her?

"Go," he said. "I'm not going to hurt him. Like you, I need answers, too." But right then and there, he accepted he'd never have a future with her, because she'd never stop loving Daniel, dead or alive.

Marco didn't plan to play second fiddle to any man. Especially someone this cruel and calculating. Reminded him too much of his own drunk dad, taunting his mother. Taunting Marco.

Calling them both names. No. He'd get this done and be on his way.

Right now, he had to protect Amelia and Samuel. "Go. Now."

So he waited until Samuel and Amelia took off toward the house, then fired a few shots in the vicinity of the man's head, missing on purpose. He also didn't want to outright kill another human being. He'd had enough of that with being in the military. Even one who had a lot of secrets floating around him. But he did want to grab that man by his collar and let him know he'd caused a whole passel of trouble.

More shots fired and then, nothing. Marco glanced around to see Samuel and Amelia safe at the corner of the porch, but when he turned and squinted through the scope again, the man was gone.

He stood, ready to get shot at again.

Still nothing happened.

He took off toward the house and reached Amelia and Samuel. "I think he left or he's on the move. Let's get out of here before he hits one of us with a bullet."

They each hurried to their vehicles.

"I'll meet y'all at the Triple R," Samuel said. "I am not a drinking man, but I sure could use one right now."

Marco made sure the area was secure and got Amelia into his truck as quickly as possible. Then he turned to her. "I don't get it. If this man loves you, why is he harassing you? That can't be right."

She glanced toward the stables. "You used the word

doppelgänger earlier. I've heard stories of people who take on other people's identities, and if Kent is out of town, could this person be staying here under false pretenses?"

"But everyone knows Daniel is dead," Marco said. "And he was an only child, right? No brothers who'd look like him."

"No. Kent and Rhoda had no other children. She left when Daniel was a teenager." Amelia watched the barn off in the distance, and then said, "But he and his mother weren't that close. I think she was bitter and miserable, and she took it out on him a lot."

"So he wasn't close to either parent?"

"No. Not close like I was to mine, or how I felt about Leo and Siri."

"So we can't get to Kent Parker just yet without a trip to New Mexico and that's iffy, and the man who's impersonating Daniel is off into the wind again."

"We could search the barn and stables before we leave."

"Nope. Too dangerous for you. We might get ambushed."

He cranked the truck and they headed out.

Amelia glanced back. "That barn is close to where the two ranches merge near the river. Not that far from the cave. That's why we heard a motor cranking the other day, when we came out on the other side of the cave. Do you think he saw us and left? Or maybe he was coming to confront us, and we got to our side without that happening?"

"A little of both, probably. But I think he's doing all of this, setting fires for distractions, hitting people over the head, sneaking into your room, because he wants to get you alone to talk. Or he wants to get you alone to kill you. Either way, he's not gonna get close to you while I have breath in my body."

Amelia gave him a measured glance, showing she'd heard the steel behind that declaration. "That scares me almost as much as he does, Marco. I can't bear something happening to you. I won't let it happen."

"I feel the same regarding you," he replied. "I'm in it now, Amelia. All in. I want this person done and gone." Then he could be done and gone and trying to forget her.

She stared over at him, the look in her eyes telling him things neither of them were ready to hear.

They made it to the spot where Daniel had died. Then Marco heard a loud pop, and the truck went spinning out of control. Someone had just shot out one of the tires.

SEVENTEEN

"Hold on," he shouted as the tires screeched against the old road and the truck went into a spin. He held the stirring wheel and guided it, letting it get over the lost tire before he brought it to a stop about a foot from the old, scarred oak. Right in front of Amelia's eyes.

She sat, her breath heaving, while she stared at the tree where Daniel had died. Then she opened the door, got out and screamed like a primal warrior. "You want me? Then show your face, you coward. Come and get me."

Marco hurried out of the vehicle and came around, his handgun leading while he scanned the woods. "Amelia, get back in the truck."

"No." She moved in a circle, her expression full of rage and pain. "Daniel wouldn't do this to me, so who are you? What do you want from me?"

No response. The trees settled, the woodland creatures retreated. Nothing. The world went still.

Then they heard a motor roaring to life deep inside the woods.

Marco hit the hood of the truck in frustration.

Amelia sank down on the ground and put her head

in her hands. That meltdown he'd been expecting was now a full-on exploding ball of pent-up rage and emotion. He could hear her sobs before he even saw her near the back passenger-side tire.

"Amelia."

He sank down beside her and let her cry. She didn't turn to him or say anything. She sat curled tight, her hands on her knees now. Her head buried against her knees, her hair wild and coming out of the messy ponytail.

"I am so angry," she finally said. "So tired and frustrated and angry and…sad. I'm just so sad. Leo is gone and I should have been here, to talk to him, to reassure him, to find out what is going on around here."

"But—"

She held up a hand, not nearly finished. "I thought when Daniel died, I'd die, too. Of a broken heart. My heart hurt so much." She gulped in a sob, her mumbled rage loud and clear. "He'd been all over the world, doing his work during some dangerous situations, and he had to come home only to die a mile from my home. Not far from his own home. How fair is that?"

Marco didn't answer. No point. She had more to say.

"And now, I'm being tormented by the *maybes* and *what-ifs*, and if that isn't enough, someone is trying to either drive me mad or outright kill me." She lifted her hand and pointed toward the woods. "That is not Daniel. You hear me out there? You are not Daniel."

Marco grabbed her hand and pulled her into his arms. "He's not. He's someone being paid to mess with you. He's not who you think he is."

She finally lifted her head, her misty eyes as green as the nearby trees. "But you—you're exactly who I think you are, Marco. Brave, stubborn, determined. You have a life and a plan for your future. But you're here with me, watching my life fall apart."

"Hey, don't you see? This is what he wants. For you to give up, give in to all that anger and all those emotions. Grief is tricky and hard, and it never goes away, but he's playing us and using us to get what he wants."

"The ranch?"

"No, Amelia. You. I think he wants you."

She pushed herself up. "And he's going to get me," she said in a loud dare of an echo that drifted through the trees like a lost breeze. "And soon."

Then she wiped her eyes and got back into the truck.

Marco took his time, doing a panoramic scan of the road and the countryside. His blood boiled with wanting to smack this person. But he was working up a hefty fee, which should make him happy. Instead, he just wanted to get Amelia back to the ranch house in one piece. It wasn't about his fee right now. He'd gladly give it up to save her.

"I'll need to change the tire," he told her through the window.

She got out. "I'll help."

"You stay inside the truck."

"I need something to do, so I'll help."

Soon they had the jack out and ready and she was taking out the lug nuts as if her life depended on it. Which it kind of did. Marco let her finish, then he lifted the shot-out tire off and put the spare on. Amelia went right back to working on the lug nuts, making sure she didn't tighten them too much until he could lever the jack down and keep the tire balanced.

"You know how to change a tire," he said, always amazed.

"I know how to do a lot of things. Comes when you live on your own. Same as you."

"Yeah, like I've said—we're a pair."

"Joined at the hip for now," she said with no animosity or spirit. Just a fact, stated as such.

He wasn't sure if that was compliment or an insult.

Soon, they were back on the road.

"I hope he heard me," she said. "I hope I hear from him."

"If you do, let me know."

"Of course."

That quick response didn't sound promising.

Marco glanced toward her. "Look, if you do murder, you won't be able to live at the ranch."

"Right now, that's not a problem."

They reached the gate and entered the long drive. He parked the truck off to the side of the four-car garage. Samuel's damaged BMW was already there.

"Look, Amelia, I know you want to draw blood, but you have to be careful. This man is obviously not thinking clearly."

"No, he's thinking all the time. He's always ahead of us, there wherever we go, which hasn't been anywhere much but across this land." She stared at the rambling stone-and-wood house, the stucco shining bright in the midday sun. "I just want to know why he thinks *he* has a claim here and *I* don't."

"Maybe he's not after the ranch. Like I said, he seems to want to get to you, any way he can. It's almost as if he's just bringing on the distractions to get your attention. And sooner or later, he'll get your attention and then he'll have you."

Amelia nodded. "Bring it." Then she got out of the truck and headed inside the house.

Rosa had Samuel sitting at the table while she checked him for injuries. "I told her I'm fine. Just my knee gave out on me. I'm not an action hero like Marco there."

"I don't think I'm quite there, either," Marco responded. "We got a flat on the road."

"Oh, really?" Alan said from across the room. "How'd that happen?"

"A rogue bullet knocked out the back tire on the driver's side."

They all looked from Marco to Amelia. She knew she looked a mess, dusty and dirty and tear stained, but she was too worked up to care right now.

"More like a carefully aimed bullet," she replied.

Alan shook his head. "This is getting out of hand."

"It ain't over till it's over," Marco said. "I hope that's soon."

"I'll make lunch," Rosa said, worry in her words.

"I could eat," Samuel replied. "Getting scared out of my boots caused me to work up an appetite."

Amelia glanced at Marco, wishing he hadn't seen her so vulnerable and emotional. Wishing so many things and wanting so many things, but she knew she had to get through this first. "I'm going to get cleaned up. Then I've got some calls to make and some other things to take care of. I want to print that one good photo I got last night."

Marco watched her go. "Good idea. I'll go and see

if I can search Ben Nesmith's house and then I'm going to check out the loft over the stables at Park Meadows Ranch. The shooter was there, waiting to scope us at the house. But he left before we did and somehow managed to get to the road and shoot at us again. We could both be dead right now, but we managed to survive yet again. I might find some clues or even the man himself there."

Amelia pivoted back around, her mind buzzing with what might go wrong. "I'm going with you."

"Bad idea," Marco said. "You need to stay here where, hopefully, you'll be safe. Each time you go out, someone tries to harm you. I can get in and out quickly and…since I don't have a warrant for either and given the fact that I'm not calling in the locals because we all know they're just sitting on this and looking the other way more than usual, I think you need to stay out of it, Amelia. I won't have you arrested for breaking and entering."

She crossed her arms, digging in, ready to protest. "Oh, but you're willing to get yourself arrested?"

"I won't get caught."

"I don't like this, Marco."

"Well, I don't like you being out there and getting shot at and terrorized."

"I've told you over and over, I can take care of myself," she retorted. "Stop smothering me."

She regretted her words instantly, but he gave her a look that for once said she might get her wish to be left alone. "Marco—"

"Okay, Amelia. You know I'm trying to protect you—and not only you—but this ranch and all the people on it, too. Think about that while I'm gone, okay?"

He turned and went out the front door, slamming it behind him.

She was about to run after him to apologize, but her phone buzzed. An unknown number. Her heart accelerating with each buzz, she moved away and looked at the phone. "I have to take this. Ranch business," she told Rosa and Alan. "I'm going to stay in my room and work on my photos for a while."

Alan nodded, but she wasn't sure she'd convinced him. "Be careful," he said. "And we'll be right here if you need us."

Amelia nodded and left the kitchen, torn between going after Marco and finding the man who was harassing her. Then she went inside, shut the door and braced herself to answer the call. Marco would take care of himself—that was his job. And she'd do the same—this was her life. She needed to hear this man, his voice, his tone, his reasoning. Or lack of reasoning. She had to see the truth with her own eyes, absorb it in her own soul, know it in her heart.

"Hello," she said, apprehension twisted up inside anticipation like a rushing river.

"You answered."

"Yes. We need to talk. Daniel, if you love me, why are you doing all these things to scare me, or do you want to kill me?"

"I'm sorry. I had to make it look bad, so I don't get taken away again. Like the night my truck went off the road."

This man knew about that night. Faking it? She pretended to believe him, but it would be easy for him to find out everything he needed to know about Daniel, Park Meadows Ranch and Rio Rojo. "So it is you?"

His voice went husky, silky, intimate. "Of course. I can't believe you'd doubt me."

"Well, I thought you were dead. Why can't you just talk to me? You know I'd let you in the front door with open arms. You know I love you and miss you so much."

"Yes, but too risky. My father always goes to extremes to get what he wants. And he wanted me to stay away."

"Where is Kent?" she asked, holding tight to her panic. What if he'd killed Kent Parker?

"He's on a trip, but you know that already, don't you?"

She had to keep him talking, to find a way to set up a meeting. "What do you want?"

"I want you. I want us. But I don't need a posse coming with you. My daddy will take me away again. That's why I've been acting so weird. I'm a grown man, you know. But he expects too much, always has."

"Daniel, you don't sound well. Are you sick? Did Kent treat you badly? Why would he send you away?"

"To keep us apart," the man said. And he sounded like Daniel. But harsh, so harsh. He couldn't be the man she once loved.

"Daniel…"

"I love hearing you call me that."

What an odd statement. "It's your name, right?"

"Yes, I just missed you so much."

"When can we meet?" she asked, checking her watch. Plenty of daylight left. She could do this. She'd take her gun and her camera.

"Yes, I'd love that. We can't talk without that shadow following us—your guard dog."

She didn't take the bait. "I'm alone right now. How about we meet at our favorite spot. Remember?"

He hesitated, which gave her a clue that he wasn't Daniel. "Yes. That's a good plan. What time?"

"One hour," she said. "I'll see you then, Daniel. I can't wait to see you by the river in our favorite place." One little hint should bring him to her side of the river, she hoped.

Another hesitation. "I'll be there." Then he added, "And if he comes with you, I will shoot to kill this time."

He ended the call and Amelia sank down on her bed, her knees wobbly. She wasn't scared of the man. But she was scared that if he was truly Daniel, someone had messed him up badly.

So badly that he didn't make sense. He sounded desperate and irrational, and extremely dangerous. But she had to know firsthand, and now was her only chance to meet him on her terms.

Hurrying, she changed into a loose tunic top that flowed out around her in vivid colors. She'd tuck her gun in the waistband of her jeans the way Leo had taught her, underneath the tank top she'd put on with the tunic.

Then she got out her smaller camera, one she could set up in the tree where she and Daniel used to meet. She'd set it on a timer to snap pictures of her with the man—for two reasons. One, she could use the pictures to identify him and prove she wasn't losing her mind, and two, if something happened she'd have proof of him being the last person she'd been seen with.

Marco would be mad, but she had to deal with this and get it done so she could decide what would happen to the Triple R. And her. She knew Marco would go in with guns blazing, and she didn't want him to die, too.

She'd get to the meeting place early, so she could watch for the man and be prepared—to find Daniel or a stranger. She'd be ready, either way. If it was Daniel, she'd talk to him. And if the man wasn't Daniel, well, she'd deal with that on her own terms, too.

EIGHTEEN

Marco parked his truck in an old battered driveway down from Ben Nesmith's empty house and hid it in the dense trees canopying what was left of the entry. Since he had no close kin, the man's house would probably just set there until some of the ranch workers could clear it out. He hoped he'd find something before anyone came by and spotted him. And he prayed Amelia would stay in the ranch house and get some rest.

His gut told him fat chance on that one. He kept praying, his silent words wafting through his brain in a cycle that kept him going.

He went to the back door and found it unlocked. No crime scene tape. Someone else had broken that down and moved on into the house. Law enforcement or somebody needing to look, too?

He pulled out his gun and entered, causing the door to creak in pain. The house was a mess, stuff thrown here and there, cabinets open with broken dishes everywhere. Someone had been here, no doubt. Had they found any evidence?

The bedroom looked even worse. Everything tossed and rearranged. After searching the closet and the one dresser, he thought about where a man might hide something he needed to keep a secret.

Marco got down on the dusty floor and looked under the bed. Nothing there. Then he got up and shoved the old bed across the room. And noticed a plank that looked higher than the others.

"Ah," he said to himself as he tapped it with his foot. An old trick, but one people often forgot when in a hurry and searching illegally.

The odd plank, about a foot long and half that wide, was loose. He pried it open with his pocketknife and found a small tin box. Like a money box. Checking outside, he didn't see anyone. So he sat down in a chair by the window and opened the old lock on the box. Easy with a twist of his knife.

Inside he saw a wad of cash—mostly one-hundred-dollar bills, and a note. "You'll get the rest when it's done." Then he spotted a photo, turned facedown, the name *Diego* written in a scratchy handwriting.

Marco lifted the old bent photo out and turned it over.

The young man staring intently into the camera looked like Daniel Parker. Marco had looked at too many pictures of the man Amelia loved. He'd always remember this man's face.

"Diego," Marco whispered. "A nickname?" He turned the picture back over and studied the landscape behind the man. It wasn't the Hill Country. A mesa, wide and hard-edged, dry. The kind of backdrop you might find in New Mexico.

"Diego," he said again. Could it be a code? He pulled out his phone and looked up the origin, just one of the tricks he'd learned over the years. "James, Jacob."

Diego was another form of those two names. It also meant *supplanter*—as in someone who illegally seizes the place of another; offender, claim jumper.

Well, that was interesting.

He put the money and note back and kept the picture.

Ben Nesmith had been hired for a job, but he hadn't completed that job. Why did he have this picture?

Marco checked around a little more, hid what he'd found where he'd found it and left, headed to Park Meadow Ranch to see what or whom he could find there. But then it hit him—he needed to search Siri's studio. Some of the artwork he remembered from Amelia's lake house had highlighted Santa Fe, New Mexico. He backed the truck around toward the Rio Rojo. He'd check there before he went back to Park Meadow Ranch, because he wanted to have all the backup information he could find before he hunted down the man who seemed to want all of them dead.

Sneaking out wasn't that hard. Marco hadn't returned yet. Amelia made sure Rosa had gone to her suite to take a nap, too. Alan had been in the office when she'd checked the whole house over, but got called down to the stables, so Amelia asked him if Puff could trot along to get some air and exercise. No way she could let the dog go with her. She went out the door from her room to the courtyard, making sure the drapes were drawn in Rosa and Alan's suite. Checking to see if any guards were hovering. Marco would have thought of that. She saw one man strolling with a rifle but managed to dodge him as she slid behind a cropping of thick bur oaks mushrooming together near the corner of the yard.

Then she darted into the woods by the pasture and kept moving until she reached the river and headed east. Glancing around, she made sure no one was following her. When she heard a motor cranking off in the distance, her heart flipped and for a brief moment, she thought about turning around. And she thought about Marco. He'd always been right there with her before. Maybe this was a bad idea. No, the man had told her to come alone. He'd shoot Marco in an ambush, so she had to do this and get it over with.

She could at least get a good look at the man, if nothing else, and then sneak back the way she'd come. She hoped her camera setup would work, too. If she panicked and left and he called again, she'd be honest and say she got scared. Why didn't she ask him to meet her on a busy street in town, or at least closer to the house? She listened to the off-road four-wheeler moving through the woods. Then the motor went silent across the narrow river bend. She couldn't hide in the cave, so she ran past it and found the spot where she and Daniel used to sit on the big rock behind an old live oak that had grown even bigger now. The trunk would hide her. She could decide then if she wanted to talk to the man.

She quickly set up the camera on the bendable tripod, standing it on a sturdy branch that allowed plenty of space for the camera to be angled down to capture her and the man as long as they stayed near the tree. Finished, she waited, hidden behind the oak where two limbs gave her about a three-inch V to watch the curve and the cave. He should be coming this way anytime now. But he didn't. She couldn't hear any footsteps or see any sign of bushes moving. The woods were quiet and still, and her breathing was low and shallow.

She held to the branches and peeked until her neck got tired. Either he wasn't coming, or he was somewhere doing the same thing she was doing—watching and waiting. She would wait ten more minutes and then she'd run back toward the house.

Her phone buzzed at about the same time she heard footsteps approaching. Looking at the caller ID, she saw Marco's number.

She shut the phone off, deciding too late this *had* been a bad idea.

Because when she turned around to go back home, the man who looked like Daniel was standing five feet in front of her, with a gun aimed straight at her heart.

Marco went inside the ranch house and found the place quiet. He checked Amelia's room, thinking she might be asleep. Her door was shut. He didn't knock, memories of their earlier words to each other still messing with his head. Better to do this search on his own since his call to her earlier had gone to voice mail. He'd wake her if he found something. She might be awake anyway and just ignoring him. He'd talk to her about that later. Now, he moved down the hallway and took a right past the office and the primary bedroom suite.

Then he found the pocket doors that opened to the studio, a large sunny room with windows all around and a stone patio off to one side, a view of the countryside all around. That was nice, but he forgot the view and started searching through paintings and drawings, instinct telling him something was going on here that would make sense once he pieced it all together.

After about fifteen minutes of rummaging through paintings of Santa Fe, Albuquerque, Hill Country vistas and landscapes, he found a portrait-sized white canvas envelope bag hidden down underneath the stacked paintings.

He hurriedly popped the snap and gently tugged at the sketch inside. When he saw it fully, Marco grunted and let out a breath. It was an etching of Daniel, looking at a mirror image of himself. Only there was no mirror. But off in the corner, barely readable, he saw where Siri had signed the sketch and added the number *2* by her name.

Daniel.

Diego.

Two.

Twins.

Marco's brain lit like a firecracker. The obvious had been right there before their eyes, just as Gregory Tyson had said. Daniel had a twin brother who must have lived in New Mexico with their mother. And Leo had been sending money to them all these years.

Could Diego be Leo Colón's son? If so, that could mean Daniel had been his true son, too. Why else would Diego be after Amelia? Maybe there was a better explanation—that Leo was a good man and had helped Daniel's mother because Daniel loved Amelia.

But again, Marco's gut told him the truth was right there in front of him. And it had been there all the time.

Not only that, but Leo and Siri had known it and accepted it. While Kent Parker had known it and hadn't accepted it so well. Or maybe he hadn't known but had somehow found out since Daniel's death. Had he brought in Diego to fight for the ranch, because Daniel had missed out on his legacy? Maybe that's why he fought so hard to keep Daniel in Texas, and also resented Amelia living the life his "son" should have had. Yet he couldn't tell Daniel the truth. But Diego—well, that would be a different story. Leo was gone and now Diego could lawfully inherit. If Amelia was out of the way. Marco had to wonder where Kent Parker was. On a trip or tucked away under Diego's command? Or worse?

Had Diego killed Kent?

What mattered now—Amelia was paying the price for their secrets.

"Not anymore," he said, hurrying to her room to alert her.

After he'd knocked several times, he didn't wait for an answer. He opened the door. "Amelia, we need to talk."

But Amelia was nowhere to be found.

"Hello, Amelia," the man said, moving toward her in a slow creeping stroll. "We finally meet."

Amelia had to blink and take a deep breath. "Daniel?"

After studying him in the light of day, she knew this wasn't the man she'd loved and lost. He did look a lot like Daniel, but his features, just like his voice, were cold and hard-edged, etched in a bitterness that made him look dangerous and a bit deranged.

And now, he had her right where he wanted her. She didn't dare glance up at her camera. But it should be recording this right now.

"You know I'm not Daniel. I was there the night he died, and I saw you. You screamed his name over and over. I was so tempted to turn around and become Daniel, but I decided to bide my time and get what I wanted another way. I've wanted to meet you since that night, but circumstances kept me away."

She realized she was caught in a vicious nightmare.

So the man she'd seen had been real, both then and now. This man had been on the road that night. Her stomach roiled and bile rose to her throat as she thought about Marco telling her sometimes the suspect came back to watch everyone and admire his work.

"Did you kill Daniel?"

His eyes looked sad while his smile looked pleased that she'd figured it out. "Well, not technically. But when you're driving on a dark road and come face-to-face with your twin, I mean… It happens. He skidded to keep from hitting me. End of story. A tragic end, though, wasn't it?"

"No, I don't believe you." She shook her head, not wanting to hear what he was telling her, the hidden gun warm against her backbone, her cell phone in a deep pocket of her jeans. She could easily kill him right now, but she wanted to see him taken away to suffer for all he'd done to her family. "Who are you?"

"I'm the other son. Diego," he said, almost spitting each word out. "Diego Parker. The one no one knew about until…until I decided to show the world the real heir to this ranch."

"This ranch? What do you mean? You're Daniel's twin? Is Kent your father?"

"Ha, that's what they all wanted the world to believe. Kent thinks he can become my father even after all these years, but he's wrong on that. I had to send him on a wild-goose chase so I could get to you."

"I don't understand," she said, trying to buy time. "If you're Kent's son, why are you harassing me?" Her mind couldn't process what her heart was telling her. Daniel had a brother, a twin, and that twin was tormenting her now?

"Sure, nobody ever understands, do they?"

"Can you tell me the whole story?"

"Yeah, but not here. That PI will come looking for you soon enough. But by then, it'll all be over."

He motioned for her. Then he looked up and straight into the tiny camera. His dark eyes flared. Grabbing her, he said, "Get that thing down, now."

"No," she said. "I had to protect myself. This is proof."

He held her against his chest and used his gun hand to shake the limb. "Do as I say, or you won't live to show proof to anyone."

Amelia took down the camera, but instead of giving it to him, she tossed it out into the weeds near the river. "Gone," she said.

They heard a noise—a siren maybe?

"That was a mistake," he said. "The first of many, but you're coming with me."

She stood still, knowing if she went with him, she'd never see the light of day again. "I'm not going anywhere with you. You can tell me the truth right here and now."

He shook his head, disappointment coloring his threats. "Sorry, sweetheart, I'm the bad twin, you see. I can kill you right here and you'll never know the truth, and I'll have to kill your precious PI, and the other people standing in my way. That couple that stays in the main house like they own it—they'd be next after that smug private investigator. Or you can come with me, and I'll explain and hey, you might even decide you like me. I like you and that's why you're still alive. Together, we can work this out."

"I doubt that," she said, remembering Marco's words to her earlier. She'd done it this time—put everyone in danger. She had no choice but to go with him. "But you're right. You wanted to see me and now here I am."

"Let's go," he said, grabbing her arm, his fingers digging into her flesh like a hot branding iron.

Nope, this hadn't been a good idea, but at least now she could find out the truth. One way or another.

NINETEEN

Marco rushed through the house, his phone tuned to 911. "Rosa, Alan?"

Rosa came out of the far hallway and hurried to the kitchen. "Marco, what's wrong?"

He gave the dispatcher the information—the ranch address, a missing woman, possibly kidnapped. A description of the unknown man and possible location of the kidnapping.

He told the dispatcher he had to hang up, so he could search. Then he explained to Rosa. "I can't find Amelia. I know who's after her."

"She was in her room," Rosa said, glancing around, her hand on her heart. "I don't hear Puff—he went with Alan to the stables."

"Where did she go?" Marco stopped, took a deep breath. "She got a phone call. Do you know who called her?"

"No," Rosa replied. "She said she'd take the call and then rest, and told me I should, too."

They both looked at each other, realization taking hold. "Are you saying she's been kidnapped?" Rosa asked, her hand going to her heart.

"Yeah, you have the same feeling I've had all day. I

knew better than to leave her alone, but I was frustrated, and she was so angry. I'm afraid Amelia's gone after the man she thinks is Daniel. And I can prove he's not."

"Who is he, then?" Rosa asked.

"Diego, Daniel's twin brother. If he lured her out, he has her now."

Rosa sank down on a stool and said something in Spanish. Marco was pretty sure it was a prayer.

Marco was about to leave, but he turned back. "Do you know about him?"

Rosa shook her head. "No, but we'd heard things— Siri and Leo talking about Kent and his ex-wife, and the problems they'd caused. Once I came up on them arguing about the *boy*. I didn't know what boy they could be talking about, maybe Daniel. Leo worried about Amelia's love life a lot. It never made sense until now, but obviously Rhoda Parker has a lot of secrets."

"Rhoda is their mother?"

"Yes, but she is dishonest and evil. She tried to come between Leo and Siri."

"I think one of her sons took after her." He didn't mention that Leo could be their father. He'd explain that later.

Rosa nodded, her eyes full of shock. "We never heard anything more about the boy, but we don't repeat that kind of stuff, you know. Personal things, and really it was years ago, but now that you mention a twin, that makes sense. Siri was a good woman and she put up with a lot, more than any of us realize, I think."

"And when you first saw the man standing outside, did any of this come to mind?"

Rosa gave him a direct stare. "No, because they were careful when we were around and never mentioned names. We shrugged it off." She lowered her head. "So many bits and pieces are coming back now. Perhaps they feared for Amelia because Daniel had a twin?"

Alan came in and took one look, Puff on his heels. "What's wrong?"

"Fill him in," Marco said. "Puff, come with me, boy. We need to find Amelia."

He took the dog and headed back to Amelia's room, grabbing some of her clothes. "Sniff."

The dog sniffed the garments, then barked. "Let's find Amelia," Marco said, glancing around. Her tote was still there, but he couldn't find her gun. Then he went to the slider door and saw the heavy wedge there had been moved to the side, slanted against the wall. The doors slid open easily.

Had she left by herself, or did someone force her?

"Did she go this way?" he asked Puff, praying the spry little mixed-breed dog would lead the way.

Puff sniffed the air and barked, then he took off through the courtyard. Marco followed, checking the magazine on his gun. Plenty of ammo. It was no surprise when Puff started off to the east toward the river.

Diego took her to the barn loft but stopped in the grass behind the stables, turning to check the woods and the parking area.

"We won't stay here. They'll come looking. You know, you and that PI, and Leo's stupid lawyer, too, really shouldn't trespass on my daddy's land. But you are trespassing, both here and on the Rio Rojo. It all belongs to me."

"Not yet," Amelia said, surprised he hadn't taken her

phone or frisked her for a weapon, surprised that just because he was Daniel's brother, he should somehow get her land, too. "I don't know how you think killing everyone in sight can possibly make you the heir of the Triple R."

He scoffed and chuckled. "I'll be the last man standing, of course. And once I explain things to poor, disillusioned Kent, he will finally see my worth."

Amelia could see this man wasn't well. He'd ranted to her even as he forced her through the cave. While he went on and on about trying to get her alone and how he'd been hampered at every turn, she stomped in the mud and, using the toe of her boot, tried to carve out an arrow pointing to this side of the river. He did stop and grab her, staying behind her.

"I tripped on a root," she said, and he kept on talking in his harsh, direct way, telling her all the reasons he had to come back here and get this business cleared up.

When they reached the walkway to the loft, she managed to loosen her beloved bracelet, and while he ranted, she dropped it by the steps leading up to the loft. Again, thankful for the big puffy sleeves on her tunic, which had hidden the bracelet and allowed her to open the clasp.

Amelia glanced down once and saw the bracelet twinkling in the sunshine. Someone had to find it here.

Now, while Diego shoved her up the steps to the loft, Amelia prayed Marco would show up as he'd told her earlier, to do a search here. But then, she changed that prayer, asking God to keep Marco away. Diego would shoot him the minute he entered the yard.

"Daddy won't believe I did all of this."

Diego's words now caught her attention even more. "You're doing all of this to impress Kent?"

Diego shoved her into a chair, giving her time to study the room and come up with her own plan. Then shock took over again. He had pictures of her plastered to the walls, pictures of her at the lake house on Caddo, her and Marco, the night of the fire there. The fire at the ranch and Marco carrying her out of the stables, blood all over her raw hands and arms. Pictures of her up close and some blurry and far away. He'd used a zoom lens on some of them. How long had he been watching and waiting?

This man would not let her live. If he couldn't have her, he'd kill her and try to take the ranch.

That's the only way he'd get it and even then, he wouldn't get away with it. Right now, she wanted to save the Rio Rojo from this psychopath.

She felt the steel of her gun underneath the gathered material of the heavy cotton empire-style tunic. That had worked only because Diego obviously didn't expect her to be carrying a weapon. And he either hadn't thought about her phone or didn't care. Her phone could be tracked easily enough. But she prayed the authorities would handle that.

Marco couldn't come here. Diego would kill him. He'd die without knowing how she really felt about him. Him, and only him. And not just because she now knew Daniel wasn't alive. She would have chosen Marco because he was different and exciting, and a good man. They'd had an instant bond, a chemistry. She'd always love Daniel, but she was in love with Marco. He'd never believe that. And why could she blame him? Daniel surrounded her thoughts day and night and she'd indicated she still wanted him back, still loved him. Right now, she had to focus on protecting Marco. And Rosa and Alan, too. Maybe even Kent.

Which made her a bit reckless. She would not let this interloper destroy what little happiness she had left.

"Why wouldn't I want to impress the old man?" Diego asked, his dark eyes smoldering with rage after he shoved her down into a chair. "He's the daddy I never knew about, not my real dad, of course, but at least he welcomed me when I found him three years ago."

Amelia shot him a hard stare. "You found Kent right after Daniel died? So you purposely caused Daniel's death and then what, just walked up on the porch and said, 'Hi, Dad?'"

Diego sat down on a bar stool in the galley kitchen, his gun still on Amelia. "Let me explain. My mother, Rhoda, was married to Kent Parker when she had an affair with Leo Colón."

Seeing the shock in her eyes, he went on. "That's right. Your dear, upright guardian was also guarding a deep secret." He smirked and then he chuckled. "But poor old Kent didn't know that at first. She told him she was pregnant, but then she picked a fight with him and left for a few months. Since she'd done that before, he waited and worried. She went back to Santa Fe and had the baby." He stopped, letting that sink in. "Wait, I mean she had two babies, but she didn't want either one of them. She didn't want her own two sons—twins."

Amelia gasped, put a hand to her mouth.

"I know, right?" He laughed. "It's shocking, isn't it?" He held up the gun and waved it around. "But wait, there's more."

He laughed, but Amelia saw the moisture in his

eyes, and the haze of a demented mind. "So she comes home to Kent and begs him to take her back. And like a lovesick puppy, he does. He takes her and her son Daniel back, thinking Daniel is really his. Or maybe he was too stupid to care who she'd been with. He just wanted an heir. So she made sure he got Daniel."

Amelia's mind went to work, but she couldn't grasp the truth just yet. Diego stared at her, the rage in his eyes pouring out in his dark expression and his irrational actions.

"Have you figured it all out, sweetheart?" he asked in a low, crawling voice.

"Why didn't she bring both of you home?" Amelia asked, the horror of this slamming her like a hammer.

"Because she sent me to live with a relative in Albuquerque. A mean relative who beat me and made me do all the chores around his stinking little ranch."

"Why would she leave Daniel with Kent and send you away? What kind of mother does that?"

He lowered his head. "The kind that isn't fit to be a mother. Rhoda wanted what Rhoda wanted, and with Kent, she got it. He loved her too much to say no. He loved Daniel and protected him, as you well know, and yet she was afraid he wouldn't want two boys who didn't really belong to him. She used him long enough to let him bond with Daniel and then she left again, and she used me to get money from Leo, who also wanted an heir. Only, he couldn't recognize that heir. He loved Siri more than he loved his twin sons."

Amelia couldn't believe what he'd told her. "But things went wrong for everyone."

Diego bobbed his head. "Kent and Rhoda had a major fight when Daniel was a teenager. She blurted out the truth, and of course, left again. From then on, Kent knew he'd been tricked and that's why he didn't want you and Daniel to get married. He didn't want Daniel to have anything to do with the Triple R."

Amelia could see it all so clearly now. "He was jealous that Daniel spent more time with me at the Rio Rojo than he did at Park Meadow."

Diego hit the counter so hard, she jumped. "Not just you, but jealous that Daniel spent time with the man who was his real father, the good, kind, generous Leo Colón. Leo, who paid my mother a hefty sum to take care of me, to keep her quiet. I saw none of that money, understand. I was with my uncle, and she sent a few hundred dollars a month to him, to take care of me. And guess what he did with the money? He used it to stay drunk." He wiped at his face. "She'd bring me home only when Leo came to visit with me, but she kept sending me away, telling people I was difficult, too hard for a single mom to handle. Daniel had been the golden boy, and me, I turned out to be the black sheep. She made me what I am today, you understand."

Amelia's fear misted into a true sympathy for this man. She could almost forgive him, but she couldn't forget all he'd done. He needed help and he'd go to jail for his crimes. Marco would figure this out, even if Diego killed her. "Diego, I'm so sorry. I can see why you're so upset."

He leaned close, no kindling of kindness in his dark eyes, so like Daniel's, and now, so like Leo's eyes. How could she have been so deceived? How did she not see this? Did everyone know but her?

"Then I hope you understand why I have to kill you," Diego said, his whisper close to her ear. "I don't want to because you're so beautiful and Daniel loved you. I know that even if I didn't get to know my brother." He lifted his hand. "I like to take pictures, too. Pictures of people, pictures of the revenge I'm trying to get on certain people."

"Like me?" she asked. "Coming to my home on Caddo Lake, shooting at me, burning down my house."

He scoffed. "I was there first and about to make my move when that overconfident PI showed up. I'd seen him slinking around the ranch, hanging out with stupid Samuel. So yeah, I followed him, figuring they'd both be looking for you. Not me. No one wanted to look for Diego." He stopped, took a deep breath. "When you came to the door, and I saw how beautiful you were, I panicked. So I tried to kill him so I could get to you."

Amelia swallowed the bile of that confession and looked him in the eye. "And when that didn't work, you set fire to my home."

"Yep. I was really angry." Then his voice turned soft and coaxing. "But I regretted that and planned to help you—bring you home. Only you took off with him instead. That doesn't work for me, Amelia."

When he touched a hand to her hair, Amelia gritted her teeth so she wouldn't cringe. She might be able to talk him down and get away from him. She prayed for that end, and she prayed for this man who'd once been a scared little boy—abandoned and used, and unacknowledged by both his parents.

"You are beautiful," he said again. "You and I—we could make the Rio Rojo even bigger and better. We'd merge it with Park Meadow, and we'd rule all this land for miles and miles."

He stood back. "Think about your choices here, Amelia."

Amelia thought about a lot of things but being with him was not on her list. "So you're saying if I don't agree to this, you'll kill me?" she asked, Marco's words running through her head.

He wants you, Amelia.

"I'm giving you the one thing you've lost, Amelia. Daniel. I can become Daniel. I've read all his journals, all the letters you wrote to him. How you visited him at college and how he did the same with you. The travels, the places you both went. I've even seen your photography, in his room at the ranch."

Diego ran his hand down her arm, then lifted her chin with his fingers. "Could you love me the way you loved him if I try to be more like him? That would save you and it might save me."

Amelia realized even more now, she would never get away from this man alive. She'd have to kill him to protect herself and everyone she loved. It would be like losing Daniel all over again, but what other choice did she have? Diego had suffered at the hands of his parents. She had to wonder if Siri knew. Did Kent know Diego's plans, or was Diego going to present her and the Rio Rojo to Kent like a gift—dead or alive?

His hand moved over her neck. "Can we agree to do this—to become the people we need to be? I can get back what's rightfully mine, and you can have the man you have always loved."

When she didn't speak, he leaned close, his face covered with sweat, his eyes full of a madness she couldn't comprehend. "Do you want that, Amelia? Or do I need to kill you and get it over with?"

TWENTY

Marco followed Puff to the cave. The dog barked and sniffed, then he kept running from the cave's opening to Marco, over and over. They heard motors roaring up at the house.

"Cavalry has arrived," Marco said. Puff barked in reply and went back to the cave entry.

"That makes sense," Marco said, hoping he'd have backup soon. He'd texted Alan to send the authorities this way. "He'd take her through the cave to get her off Triple R land fast."

Marco sure wasn't going to wait around for their backup to find them. Texting Alan again to say he thought they'd taken the cave, but they needed to check the whole area around the cave and the river, he patted the anxious dog on the head. "Let's go, Puff."

They entered the narrow cave, the warm temperature falling ten degrees as a dank, musky smell assaulted Marco's nostrils. The darkness took a minute to get used to, but Marco couldn't wait for his eyes to adjust.

He held his high-powered flashlight up and then moved it down, seeing nothing. Puff sniffed here and there, but the dog kept going back to one spot. The same spot where he and Amelia had seen boot prints the other day.

Marco quickly flashed his light to where Puff had sniffed over and over. Definitely fresh footprints, but one indention stood out from the others. It looked like a rough arrow pointing to the Park Meadow side of the river.

Marco's pulse rose as he bent down and held the light steady so he could be sure. Puff woofed and did circles. "Good boy," Marco said. "I think Amelia left us a clue."

He checked it again from every angle. The long straight muddy line with two tented marks indented on each side looked like an arrow pointing straight ahead. How she managed this, he'd never know. As long as she was alive, he didn't care. He got that they'd gone this way.

"Let's go, Puff," he said. "But we have to be quiet now."

He hadn't thought about the dog barking an alert. But he couldn't make Puff go home now. He didn't have time to worry about that.

Marco and the dog made it through the cave and out the other side, where fresh footprints had indented the grass on a worn trail through the pasture and woodland.

Marco studied the footprints, one hard and with rigid impressions. The other indented with flower imprints. A woman's boot tracks, no doubt. And Amelia's old tan boots had flowers etched in the leather. Puff sniffed here and there but seemed determined to get to where Amelia might be.

Marco felt the same way. Why had he left her alone? He knew she was bold and impulsive, and yet, he'd walked out and left her, thinking to protect her, and thinking that by now she'd know to sit tight until they could meet back up. Had she picked a fight with him deliberately? She had received a phone call. Only one thing would have made her leave the house—if she thought she could talk to Daniel alone.

He promised himself when he found Diego, he'd punch him in the face first and ask questions later. Diego had obviously lured Amelia out of the house, and she'd somehow gotten past the guard Marco had watching her room.

None of that could be changed now. He kept hurrying through the path, finding broken branches here and there. When he reached the thicket surrounding the main house at Park Meadow, he held Puff and patted the dog's head. "Hush up now. You can't bark. Quiet."

Puff whimpered and did a low growl. Maybe Ben Nesmith had trained the dog properly because Puff did understand commands.

"Good boy."

Marco followed the edge of the woods past the herd of longhorns and the beautiful horses grazing in the corral. Someone had been taking care of things, but where was Kent Parker?

And where were Diego and Amelia?

Marco and Puff finally arrived at the edge of the big yard where the stables were located. No workers lived on this property, which meant they came and did their work and left as needed. So he couldn't count on finding anyone this late in the day. Diego had probably planned it that way.

They rounded the corner of the barn where the loft was located. Puff barked, but Marco held him and quieted him. The dog sniffed and whined. Marco glanced around, the last of the sunset sharpening the angles in a golden light. He watched the door and the windows, hoping to catch a glimpse of Amelia, but the blinds were shut tight, and the door the same. He checked the steps, thinking he could hide there.

Then his eye caught something glistening in the grassy weeds. "Shh," he told Puff. The dog got quiet as they slipped from building to building until Marco was near the steps. He glanced down again, his heart flatlining before he regained his pulse.

Amelia's bracelet. Either she'd lost it in a struggle, or she'd left it here on purpose. Because she rarely went anywhere without her bracelet. Marco picked it up, thinking of how she held to the charms when she was agitated, remembering how she always put it on her bedside table each night and put it back on each morning. He remembered cleaning this bracelet when she'd gotten hurt a few days ago.

Turning it over, he stared at the circular charm with the oak tree etched in it—the tree of life. Then he studied the engraved initials—DP and AG. It had a double side. When he flipped it over, he was surprised to see two *Ds* on each side with a bigger *P* in the middle. Daniel Parker? Or had someone put the truth right there on her bracelet. Daniel and Diego Parker.

He had to find her and tell her the truth. Not just the truth about Daniel and Diego and this whole mess, but the truth of him falling in love with her. He hadn't been sure before, but now, no matter what was still between them, he wanted her to know how he felt. What if he never had an opportunity to tell her that?

He placed the bracelet in his jeans pocket and hurried up the steps, careful to stay quiet. Puff seemed to understand but the dog growled low, as if he smelled someone he didn't like. Marco didn't hesitate. He kicked the door in and rushed inside.

And saw the walls lined with photos of Amelia. Even photos from Caddo Lake. This man had been watching her long before Marco got there. Pushing that to the back of his brain, Marco searched the whole place. Nothing. No one.

He came back out to the landing, Puff at his heels. Where had they gone? Then he heard a gunshot. Coming from the main house.

Marco took off running, the dog behind him barking with each step. No time to do anything but get to Amelia. He didn't want to think about what might be going on inside that house, but he knew he had to get there before it was too late.

Amelia kept her gun on Diego. She'd missed his heart, but his arm was bleeding. "I'll have better aim next time," she warned him. "I agreed to come here so we could talk in private, but I'm tired now, Diego. This isn't working for me."

Diego lifted his gun in what had become a showdown, ignoring the blood trickling down his left arm. "You shouldn't have done that, Amelia. How can I trust you now?"

"I can't trust you," she shouted, her mind roiling with everything he'd confessed to her earlier. She'd pulled out her gun without thinking, ready to end this.

Kent was with Rhoda? She'd kept him busy, wooing him to fall in love with her again? The poor man had no idea what was going on at his ranch. He'd left the foreman in charge, but Diego was now calling the shots. So that could mean the foreman had been dismissed or, worse, was dead.

"Kent won't come home for a while. He can't until I'm ready to tell him the news," Diego told her once they were inside the main house. "We'll keep moving until you make your decision."

She'd talked him down earlier, telling him she needed more time to adjust since he looked so much like Daniel. "I think I can do this, Diego. It's the perfect plan. We can run the ranch together—you as the rightful heir and me, because I love the ranch and I think I can love you one day."

"That would be the dream." His calm tone belied the frantic nature of his movements. He was jittery and nervous, sweat pouring down his face, his shirt wet and sticking to his skin. It was hot and muggy in the house, but the air conditioner finally kicked on. She'd waited until he went to get some water and then she'd pulled her gun out and shot at him. She'd hit his left arm, but it could just be a graze.

Now, she wanted answers. He could shoot her if he wanted, but she'd shoot him back if she had no other choice.

"Did you kill him?" she asked.

Diego shook his head. "No, I don't want to kill the man. Kent did raise Daniel after all. Now I can be his son. Leo is gone. It's a no-brainer. All you'll need to do is sign the Triple R over to me. Once we're married, I'll put your name back on the deed." He moved closer. "Put the gun down, Amelia. We can talk this out. Don't make me shoot you."

"If you pull that trigger, I'll do the same," she said.

"I mean it. My whole life has changed, and you owe me some answers."

He nodded, his voice weak now. "I just want you and the ranch. You owe *me* that, don't you think?"

She would never marry this man. He had to be demented to even think that after he'd harassed her and hurt others. Killed others. She owed him nothing. But his parents and Leo had done a number on him.

So she asked, "Did you kill Leo?"

Diego waved the gun so fast, she thought he'd shoot her. But he just held the weapon and inched closer. "What do you think?"

"He died suddenly and with no known illnesses, but the body wasn't examined closely. Natural causes."

"Then that's your answer," Diego said, moving backward to a window, his gun still trained on her. "I hear a dog barking. Let's go."

"No," she said, moving toward him in a swift run.

He turned so quickly, she didn't see him coming. With a burst of strength, he knocked the gun out of her hand, then grabbed her wrist, a flinch of pain on his face, his fingers burning against her skin.

"You don't get to order me around, Amelia. Now I know you don't really want us to be together. So you'll write a note, leaving the ranch to me. Then I'll kill you."

"No one is going to let you have the ranch, Diego. Neither of these ranches. There's too much evidence against you."

"Then I'll have to keep you alive, for collateral."

She twisted around to get her gun from the floor, wanting so badly to pull the trigger. But he was too quick. He shot but hit a cabinet and cracked the door. "You'll be next," he said, grabbing her arm again.

She struggled against his bloody hand, but he managed to knock her gun away from her feet and send it flying across the room. Then he dragged her toward the back door and opened it, only to find Marco's gun aimed at him.

"Let her go," Marco said, his eyes storming with fire, his expression marked with rage.

Amelia shook her head, relief followed by apprehension. "Marco, he'll kill you."

Diego twisted her around and held her in front of him. "She's right. I'd planned on killing you anyway. Might as well be now. You can watch me shoot her first."

Marco didn't bulge. "Let her go and you can take me."

"Nope. Sorry, you're not a part of this equation. You are a nuisance, however." He moved closer, his gun in Amelia's ribs.

"You won't get far," Marco said. "We've got this place surrounded." Outside, Puff barked a sharp warning.

"All the more reason to take her with me," Diego said. "Get out of my way or I'll shoot her—I don't want to kill her because we're going to Santa Fe, and we'll be married. That should tie things up nicely. My mamma and daddy might finally be proud of me. I'll have a new bride and the Rio Rojo, too."

"I can't let you take her," Marco said, realization cresting in his gaze. "Your plan won't work. Your plan is falling apart, and you know it. I can see the desperation in your eyes."

Amelia saw the fear in Marco's eyes when he looked at her, but she also saw the love. He'd die for her. "Marco, let me go with him," she whispered. "He needs me. He won't kill me. I'll sign over the ranch, Diego. Just let Marco go."

That made Diego even madder. In one swift move, he shielded himself with her and shot at Marco. Marco shot back but over their heads. Then he fell down on the side porch near the kitchen, blood pouring a few inches from his heart.

"Marco," Amelia screamed. "Marco."

He didn't move. Puff came up and sniffed at him, then whimpered. He came running, but Diego kicked at him and missed. Puff backed up but kept barking.

Sirens sounded in the background.

"I hope they find you," she shouted at Diego. "You are an evil monster, and you'll never own the Rio Rojo. They'll have all the evidence to put you away forever."

"Shut up. I've covered my tracks. I don't exist, re-member. Besides Kent and my mother, you're the only one who even knows about me. I took care of your pre-cious PI, and that useless Ben Nesmith, too. He turned into a coward. Didn't want to murder a woman."

Amelia held the scream that echoed inside her head. While he forced her toward a waiting truck behind the garage, she tried to leave prints on everything. She had no gun now, but she still had her phone hidden in her jeans. He was injured and that meant he could lose control of the wheel. If she could get the truck off the road, she'd run through the woods.

His next words gave her hope. "You're driving," he said. "I'm hurt and I can't trust you. So you drive. I'll keep my gun on you to make sure you do as I say."

Right now, she had to calm down and get him calmed down, so she got in on the driver's side. The sun would set soon, and it would be hard to get away. She glanced back to the porch.

And saw Marco lift his head.

He wasn't dead.

Holding her breath, she glanced toward Diego. He'd been so focused on her, he hadn't noticed.

She would have to see this through to the bitter end, but she wouldn't give up on Marco.

Amelia began a silent prayer. *Lord, give me strength, and please, help Marco. Don't let him die. I need him. I need You.*

She prayed as she cranked the motor, hoping someone would find her. And she prayed that if her time was up, she'd be able to accept that and somehow forgive this madman who'd taken her for all the wrong reasons.

"Where?" she asked, tears on her face, the image of Marco lying there burning through her soul.

Diego wiped his face, smearing blood across his jaw. "I told you, New Mexico. My mother wants to meet you."

No way she'd let him take her over the state line and all the way to New Mexico to get married. Rhoda would certainly kill Amelia with her bare hands. And probably Diego, too. Amelia would find a way to stay in Texas, and to stay alive. She'd just have to keep him talking while she figured out a different route.

"How will we get there? People will be looking for me."

The sun had disappeared as a dark cloud hovered overhead. She saw lightning brightening the sky inside the cloud. A storm was coming.

In the sky.

And in her heart.

Diego glared at her. "Will you stop asking questions?"

"But I need to know more, Diego. You look so much

like Daniel, and you know so much about me. I want to learn more about you. Tell me about Rhoda."

He laughed and waved the gun in a wild loop. "Rhoda won't get any mother of the year awards, but she'll do what I tell her, out of guilt, not love. She's taking care of Kent while I get on with business. My mother doesn't plan to miss out on my inheritance, you understand?"

"I do, I really do," Amelia said, seeing the entire plan. "But I'm not sure about all of this. I need time, Diego. Time to get used to you."

He took a deep breath. "You'll have the rest of your life with me if you do as I say. I thought we'd agreed on that."

He'd agreed. Not her, not in this lifetime.

She stalled him with her questions regarding how he'd managed to pull this off. Diego wasn't dumb. He'd planned out every detail of his attacks and he was ready to brag to her. Amelia tried to remember everything, but if he got tired and decided to kill her, no one would ever know.

Kent Parker had no idea what was happening. She understood that now. Diego had made sure of that. He'd caused Daniel's death, and he'd somehow caused Leo's death, then he'd found out where she lived, and now he wanted to marry her just long enough to gain the inheritance and then get rid of her for good.

But Diego didn't know her that well at all.

She'd survive this and see him dead or in prison.

TWENTY-ONE

Marco stood in the kitchen with a clean rag to his wound. Shoulder, shot through and through. A chair was overturned, cold food set on the counter, and blood splatters covered the floor and back door handle. Grabbing a bottle of water and some over-the-counter pain pills, he headed out the door, only minutes behind them. He coaxed Puff to go home. He couldn't waste another minute. But he would catch up.

He wasn't done with this conversation and he sure wasn't letting Diego take Amelia across the state line.

He saw the sheriff hurrying toward the house, so he filled him in on what had happened. "Diego took her hostage. I'm going after them."

"That's a bad—"

Marco didn't wait to hear the sheriff's words.

He knew the deputies would work fast, dusting for prints, taking blood samples, checking each room and searching for clues. They had enough physical evidence to get Diego on kidnapping if nothing else.

The sky lit with a lightning bolt, followed by a hard roll of thunder.

"Yeah, I know the feeling." Marco gunned the gas

and reminded himself of Amelia's strength. "She's smart. She probably left her prints everywhere."

He sped along the narrow road, going far too fast for the upcoming curves.

Then he spotted the truck stopped up ahead.

His heart went cold when he recognized the spot— where Daniel had died. Skidding in some rocks, he left his truck running and hurried to the other vehicle. It had been smashed into a tree. Not the big oak across the road, but one sturdy enough to cause damage. The motor smoked and coughed, and both doors were open.

But Amelia and Diego were nowhere to be found.

Marcus hurried to shut his truck down and grab more ammo. Then he headed into the woods and saw two sets of tracks and a few bloodstains on green leaves, his worst fears tugging at him. They'd had a head start, but he could get to them if he hurried.

He heard a dashing sound moving toward him and held his gun out. Puff came running.

"Okay, you can help," he told the dog. "And use your teeth."

He and Puff followed the footprints leading back toward the river. Marco saw the flower-shaped imprints of Amelia's boot soles and knew he was on the right track. Diego was taking her back across to her land now.

Marco made it to the river but lost the flower-shaped footprints about a fourth of a mile before the cave. A bolt of lightning crashed to the west, and then thunder rumbled. The sun disappeared behind the dark cloud. Puff barked and danced, ready to roll.

"Where did you go, Amelia?"

* * *

Amelia's eyes burned with a sandpaper sharpness while drowsiness tried to take over. She needed water. She needed a plan, a way out of this mess. She'd come close when she'd ran into the river, hoping to get away.

But Diego had hurled himself after her and dragged her into a heavy thicket of vines and weeds that tore at her wet clothes and left welts on her face and arms.

They were inside the cave.

Diego was wired, ranting at times, then turning sweet and concerned at other times, his talk ranging from the ranch to his mother, then back to Amelia marrying him.

She pushed away a shiver that could turn into a panic attack if she didn't control it. Did he actually think he could pull this off—her marrying him, letting him become Daniel? That was the plan of a madman. He was nothing like Daniel, and while she could empathize with his plight, she couldn't forgive all the things he'd done in retaliation.

She'd die trying to stop him from hurting anyone else.

"Diego," she finally said, "I'm tired and I need water."

He looked surprised, his frown as dark and raging as the cloud over the horizon. "You don't deserve water. If you try to run again, I'll call the wedding off and let you die out here."

The rain worked in Amelia's favor, no matter how tired and sleepy she was. She'd tried to escape again earlier but he caught her when she tripped over an old limb. She heard sirens coming and going, people talking and shouting. People were trying to locate them. But not many knew of the cave.

The rain had picked up and now water flowed about

six inches from where he'd forced her on a small out-cropping that looked like a narrow bench set in the middle of the cave.

Amelia kept thinking she'd find a chance to run again, but she had no weapons left and her foot hurt. She'd never make it. The river water ran swift during these downpours.

She'd risk drowning to get away from him.

"Hey, I'm the one with the gun," he reminded her, as if he could read her thoughts. "You must be thinking of that PI guy—Marcus, Milton, oh, wait, Marco. Yeah, he's a real winner."

She had to lie. "I'm only thinking of survival, because I really don't want you harassing me and threatening me," she shouted. "Now leave me alone."

Diego grunted and lifted the gun away. "You'd better behave, Amelia, if you want to live till your wedding day."

"That might be a while," she shot back.

Diego shook his head. "Oh, didn't I tell you? My mother is planning our wedding. We'll get married as soon as we can get to Santa Fe."

His laughter clattered against her nerves while a bright red warning jingled like the charm bracelet she'd left behind. What if Marco hadn't found any of her clues?

Marco would forever be grateful for fancy flower-etched cowgirl boots with special soles that left flower imprints. He'd picked up their trail again and found a broken branch.

Which one of them had tripped over it?

Now there was an APB out on Diego, and Marco

was getting closer to the cave. But the rain and darkness kept him guessing. He couldn't use his phone flashlight. It was slow going but Puff stayed with him, picking up scents here and there.

Diego must have taken her around the cave and back to Parkview Ranch. Marco stopped and listened, the rain soaking him as he prayed.

I sure could use some guidance here, Lord. Please help me find Amelia. She's a good woman and I love her. She's shown me I have to have faith, so I'm going on that.

He kept praying while he searched. He'd texted Alan and told him what happened, and that the sheriff had people going over Parkview Ranch.

Now, his phone buzzed. "Alan, tell me you've heard from her."

"Not Amelia, but you won't believe this," Alan said, out of breath.

Marco braced himself for the worst. "What now?"

"Kent Parker called, looking for Amelia. He'd left several messages earlier."

"What?"

Alan went on. "He's been with Rhoda for weeks, but not because he wanted to be there. She lured him back and things were good for a while. But he got suspicious when earlier tonight he inadvertently saw a text to Rhoda from Diego, stating, 'I have her. Get ready for the wedding. Soon Amelia Garcia will be my wife and we'll finally have both ranches.'"

Marco rubbed at his rain-wet skin. "Diego and Amelia?" He remembered Diego ranting about that. "He is seriously misguided."

"Diego and Amelia," Alan explained. "Kent took

the boy in a few months after Daniel died but kept it on the downlow. Diego told him he didn't want his mother to find him, and Kent was still in shock from losing Daniel."

"Only Rhoda knew all along?" Marcus guessed.

"Apparently," Alan said. "When Kent confronted her, she told him they could all be together again and that Diego would get his inheritance, that the Triple R was his by right."

"So Kent is clueless in all of this?"

"Yes, he'd fallen for her tricks all over again and planned to remarry her. But she didn't want to move back here just yet. She got him to Santa Fe by telling him she was worried about Diego. Before he left the ranch, Kent and Diego had a horrible fight and Diego told him it was all Rhoda's fault that he was so messed up. Kent left to find out the truth. They both played him."

Marco let that sink in. "So what is Kent going to do?"

"I don't know. He's not answering his phone now. His plane was about to land. He said he'd be here soon. I'm worried about him. Kent was going to call someone to alert the Texas authorities. I told him we were aware, and that Diego has Amelia."

"And?"

"He only asked that we don't kill Diego."

"I might not be able to keep that promise," Marco said. "My goal is to save Amelia."

He ended the call and hurried back on his trek toward the cave. He'd start there and keep looking, and if he had to shoot Diego Parker, he'd do it.

Amelia had always believed in God's hand in her life. Tonight, she'd prayed for a way out and she'd managed to shoot Diego and that had weakened him. Then she'd purposely wrecked the truck to give her a chance to run away. She'd left clues here and there, and Marco had found her. He'd find her again.

She had to keep believing that. She had the image of him lifting his head and looking at her. He had to be alive.

She pictured Marco on his way to find her now. She pictured Alan and Rosa praying for her, and she pictured Daniel's smile, his words to her, *"You can do this, Amelia. I love you."*

She missed him so much. Even more now. He shouldn't have died that way. Now she needed to live—for him, for Leo and Siri, and for her parents. That had always been her goal.

Now, she thought of Marco again. He'd do everything in his power to see this through. She knew that. But she couldn't live through seeing him die.

So she had to make a move. Diego was ranting about New Mexico. They could go several ways, but he wanted the fastest one. Highway 285 could get them to Santa Fe. If they could get out of this cave without anyone seeing them. They'd have to go to the Triple R and get a vehicle. After everyone was asleep and fewer law enforcement people were around.

Amelia listened to him, and she listened to the rain, the night creatures moving through the cave, all of it making her cringe. But Diego made her cringe the most. She wasn't about to be forced into a farce of a marriage because she knew what would come next. She'd die some sort of horrible death and then Diego and Rhoda would have it all. Until their lies caught up with them.

She was about to make her move, when suddenly the choice was taken out of her hands. Puff came running into the cave, his bark aggressive, and jumped in the flowing water to swim right up to Diego. Then the wet dog jumped up and sank his teeth into Diego's leg.

Diego shouted, "Stop!" He tried to kick Puff away, but the dog held tight, its dark eyes wide. Diego cursed and screamed, "Stop, you mangy mutt. I'll shoot you!"

Amelia rebalanced herself, then grabbed at the gun Diego still held, wrestling with him while Puff went wild and showed his teeth. The dog refused to let go. Diego tried to hit Puff with the gun but dropped it. It bounced onto the outcropping and landed in a small crevice.

Muddy water soaked her boots as she stood, but Amelia bent toward the gun and grabbed it. Then she aimed it toward Diego. This time, he would not get away.

Marco had planned a surprise attack, but Puff had other ideas. He heard the dog snarling, heard a male's voice. Puff had Diego. Marco hurried in the dark, using his phone light to guide him.

"Amelia?"

"I'm here, Marco. I'm here."

He entered the cave, water rushing against his legs, and saw her standing there in the river's flow, holding a gun on Diego. Puff growled, his teeth set against Diego's dirty jeans.

"Get this mutt off me," Diego cried.

Marco motioned to Amelia. "Come here where it's safe."

She shook her head, her eyes wild in the muted light. "No."

Marco saw her pain, felt every bit of the agony she'd been through. He wouldn't blame her, but she'd blame herself. "Amelia, I have him now. You don't need to do this."

"Yes, I do," she said, her tone firm and calm. Too calm. "He's killed everyone I love."

Marco inched closer. "And he'll pay. In a jail cell for the rest of his life."

Diego struggled to stand, worked desperately to toss Puff away. "I should have killed you both that first night at the cabin."

"Yeah, you sure messed up there, didn't you?" Marco said, moving closer.

"Amelia, give me the gun."

"No. I can't let him go again."

"Puff and me, we got this," Marco said. "And the authorities are on their way."

Amelia didn't want to give up the gun. She'd worked so hard to stay alive, to have this moment. Her hand shook, the trigger cold against her fingers. Would she feel good, killing a man? Killing Daniel's twin brother? Would that bring her joy, or would it bring more despair?

She thought again of Daniel and how he ran into danger to save lives. She looked at Marco, a man who'd been willing to do the same for her. How could she ever look at him again, or look at herself in the mirror if she did this deed?

"Marco," she said, her voice weak and weary. "Help me."

Marco sprinted through the water, headed to her.

But Diego still had some fight. He kicked out just as

Marco reached the spot where Puff had Diego cornered. Marco slipped and lunged at Diego.

Amelia screamed as they went to battle. Diego tried to grab Marco's gun. Marco held tight, but he had to fight to stay standing. Puff let go and stepped back, barking and growling.

Amelia watched in horror, but because of the darkness, she couldn't take a shot. She might hit Marco.

She searched around for anything she could use. She still had the gun. Turning it where she held the barrel in her hand, she rushed to try and hit Diego over the head.

He and Marco kept at it. She screamed at them to stop. Puff kept barking.

Then she heard voices and a light shined straight into the cave. What happened next seemed to go in slow motion, but it was over in less than a minute.

A deputy stood holding a light, but a man behind him rushed forward and stared in the cave.

The next thing she knew, a shot rang out and Diego's body went limp. Marco stood by, breathing hard and looking down as Diego slid toward the water. He went to lift Diego up, but an arm pushed him out of the way.

"Let me," Kent Parker said. "I'm the one who shot him."

Amelia sat in an ambulance bay with a blanket around her. Numbness wanted to drag her down, but she had to stay alert.

Marco came and took her hand. "They're bringing him out now."

She nodded, her tears dry, her heart pounding. "I can't believe what I saw with my own eyes."

"I know, but Kent has been pushed too far this time.

He snapped. Rhoda and her son played him so they could get their hands on both Parkview Ranch and Rio Rojo. Greed turns people into nasty human beings."

She looked down at the cuts and scratches on her arms and remembered Diego's deranged rantings. "Daniel was blessed to have Kent as a father. Everyone else sure did a number on him, too. But Diego, he suffered so much, Marco. I couldn't kill him and now, Kent has to live with doing that."

Marco nodded and touched a hand to her cheek. "Yes, but he did it to save you and me, Amelia. He asked me to come and check on you. He wants to talk to you."

"Kent? What's there left to say?"

Marco looked over at the man standing there, his shoulders hunched over, his head lowered. "That's between you and him."

She nodded. "Okay."

Marco motioned to the man.

Kent came over and looked Amelia in the eye. "I'm sorry," he said, his voice gravelly. "I never knew about Diego until after Daniel died. I tried to do right by him and Rhoda. But she gets to me every time and this time, it stung hard. I thought we could become a family, but they were both using me. They took advantage of Leo's guilt, but they killed him—pesticides or something, probably in his whiskey. Leo loved his whiskey. I haven't found out yet for sure."

Amelia sat up straight. "Did Leo have an affair with Rhoda after he married Siri?"

"No," Kent said. "It was always a competition between him and me. We both spotted Rhoda at a dance hall and that was that. He had an affair with her after she and I got hitched. Looking back, I can see that once he met Siri on a trip out west, it was over between him and Rhoda. So she passed off Daniel as mine. Sent Diego away. She'd rather party all night instead of feeding babies and changing diapers."

"But she stayed with you for a long time."

"Yes, because she was waiting for the opportunity to extort Leo and she did, by picking a fight with me. She turned to him for comfort, but what she really wanted was cold, hard cash. He sent her money every month. She wanted more, but he refused, and he went to Siri and told her the truth. She was his true love, his anchor. Now they're all gone. Everybody I knew. I treated Leo so bad, and I'm ashamed of that. Same with you. I knew Daniel loved you, but I hated that he did. I was so afraid he'd find out the truth."

Amelia stood and took Kent's hands in hers. "You loved Daniel. That's all I need to know. And Kent, you saved our lives tonight. Thank you."

Kent's eyes watered up. "I'm so sorry. If he'd a-killed you, I don't think I'da made it, either."

"You have me now," she said. "And Alan and Rosa. I'll be here if you ever want to talk about Daniel."

Kent nodded and walked away, a brokenhearted man.

Amelia turned to Marco. "I guess I owe you a check."

Samuel came running. "Amelia, are you all right?"

"Perfect timing," she said. "You can pay Marco now. And give him a big tip."

"I don't mind if I do." Samuel shook Marco's hand. "You're not leaving now, are you?"

Marco looked at Amelia. "That all depends. I need to tie up some loose ends, but I might make my way back."

Amelia nodded. "I'll be waiting, cowboy."

Two months later...

Summer shimmered in rippling wheat and grazing grasses, and the Hill Country spread out in a mixture of roads, trees and water as Marco turned his truck toward the Rio Rojo Ranch.

He sat in the truck for a while, remembering when he'd kissed Amelia goodbye. A long kiss, a promising kiss.

But her last words to him didn't sound that way.

"I'll never forget you."

And he sure hadn't forgotten her.

The front door opened, and Amelia stepped out. She had on a long floral dress and a new pair of boots, etched in big bright sunflowers. She looked like a never-ending summer.

He got out and met her halfway.

"I figured you'd sit there until I dragged you inside."

"No, I was trying to find my courage, is all."

"Scared, cowboy?"

"Of you? Yes."

"I'm as tame as a kitten," she said, moving closer. Then she did drag him—into her arms. "I thought you were gone for good. I know you had big plans and you'd get on with those plans."

"I did and I still have big plans. I sold the farm and I'm flush with my own money."

"Oh, is that what this is about, you keeping me guessing? You don't like me having more money than you?"

"Didn't say that. I just like to earn my keep."

"You've done that, Marco. But...you wanted to keep your farm."

"I found something I want to keep even more," he said as he tugged her close. "You."

He kissed her, a long kiss, a kiss that felt like a lifetime of challenges and happiness. "I love you."

"I love you," she replied. "And don't worry, I'll make you earn your keep."

"I have no doubt."

"Okay, that's settled, then. Let's go eat. Rosa made tamales and a big beautiful fresh salad. She always said you'd show up one day."

"I like Rosa."

They entered the double doors of Rio Rojo and left the past outside in the shimmering heat. When they made it into the kitchen, Amelia whispered, "Oh, and by the way, I'm redoing the courtyard. It's time."

* * * * *

Dear Reader,

I've always loved Texas and so do our readers. I enjoyed setting this story there beginning in East Texas on Caddo Lake, which is one of my favorite places in the world, and moving on to a ranch near San Antonio, another fascinating Texas city.

Marco and Amelia were both in danger from the beginning, but someone wanted Amelia out of the way so they could inherit the Rio Rojo Ranch. Marco was torn between helping her or getting on with his real life.

I think that happens with us sometimes. We don't want to get involved, but we also want to do what's right. Marco had a strong sense of finding justice, and Amelia had a strong sense of protecting the place that had once been her haven. They both had to face a few truths while dealing with evil.

In the real world, evil can take over, but in this book, good won over bad and Amelia and Marco realized they are both worthy of love—for each other—and God's love for both of them. I hope if you're hurting and afraid, you'll think about that and know you are worthy!

Until next time,
May the angels watch over you. Always.
Lenora Worth

Get 4 FREE REWARDS!

We'll send you 2 FREE Books plus 2 FREE Mystery Gifts.

HARLEQUIN
PLUS

Announcing a **BRAND-NEW** multimedia subscription service for romance fans like you!

Read, Watch and Play.

Experience the easiest way to get the romance content you crave.

Start your **FREE 7 DAY TRIAL** at <u>www.harlequinplus.com/freetrial</u>.

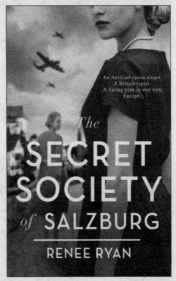